THE ROADMAN

Part 1 of 2

LeeSha McCoy

Contents

Acknowledgements
Many thanks to...
My family as always.
Beverley Paul, Leanne Rodgers and Lynda Richardson.
My Test readers, Tamara Greene, Jolene Oakey,
Glen, Mika and Fee for research purposes.

Dedicated to...
My first born son, Keontay. The blessing I waited so long for.
If you even think about becoming a Roadman, Mommy will kill you.
I love you.

Note to reader...
I have kept the UK Urban slang to a minimum in this book,
but if you would like explanations of certain words or phrases please either message
me on social media and I will explain or look at www.urbandictionary.com

CHAPTER 1

"BREAKING NEWS THIS MORNING... disorder has broken out across West London after a series of shootings and attacks..."

"Yeah, we know," I mutter to myself before swallowing my mouthful of toast and switching off the TV. All this crazy violence needs to stop—it's getting way out of control now. I check the clock on the wall. Late again. "*Shit.*"

I quickly check my face in the hallway mirror for crumbs, and after wiping under my big brown eyes and tightening my ponytail, I'm out the door to work.

I rush into the studio and cower when I see Johnny eyeing me from the front desk.

"I know, I'm sorry." *I am so late.*

His face lights up with a stunning smile as he crosses his heavily tattooed arms and leans back in his chair. "I moved your appointments, Hun. Don't worry, you have twenty minutes."

Relief washes over me. "Have I told you how much I love you lately?"

"Only every day this week. Your kit is all ready to go, can I get you a coffee?"

I flash him my blue Thermos in my bag. "Got one, thanks, Babe."

He hands me a handful of envelopes. "Here's the mail. I've paid all the invoices for the month."

"Thank you." I make my way to my domain; back left corner—that's me. I put my flask on my desk and prepare the inks for my first appointment.

"Layla?" Marco, my second in command appears. He runs a hand over his bald head—something is wrong. "I need to leave at three today, if that's cool?"

I'm surprised by his request. He never leaves early or takes time off, so of course I'm gonna say yes. "Um, how are your appointments set?"

"I've rearranged the ones affected. I know you're packed out, and I didn't wanna put any appointments on Maverick."

Thank god, I don't need any more work.

"Perfect. Thank you. Is everything okay?" I'm concerned. This is not like him at all.

His face flashes with worry. "I hope so. Let you know Monday?"

"No problem."

"Thanks, Layla." He returns to his workstation opposite mine and calls over his next customer. I hope everything is okay with him. He's been with me from the day I opened this studio and is the best tattooist I have here, after myself.

The door goes, and it's my first customer—one of my regulars, Tony. He smiles at me as Johnny books him in. It's his payday and I'm finishing his left sleeve today.

"Today's the day," he says as he reaches my station. His excitement is real.

I raise an eyebrow. "Finally."

"Well, if it wasn't so expensive..."

I glare at him and cross my arms.

"I'm joking!" he laughs. "You're worth every penny."

I bow in my chair. "Thank you."

Tony's covered in tattoos, but unfortunately, I didn't do all of his ink... I adjust my chair when he sits down and then I sterilise his arm.

"Has my friend been in to see you yet?" he asks.

"Adam? Yeah, he was in yesterday. Who inked him before? He wouldn't tell me."

"Inked 'r' us, over in East."

"Ugh, I've done so many cover-ups for them now. I don't know how they're still in business."

"You should open another shop over there."

"If only I could be in two places at once, huh?"

"If only."

My day passes quickly, it always does. I'm booked up for months in advance but I wouldn't wish it any other way. It's taken me years to get where I am today but I never gave up. Being a girl in this industry is so much harder than it is for a man, but my hard work has paid off and now I'm finally getting the recognition I deserve.

At seven I lock up the shop and head to the car park. I can hear a group of youth's fighting as I approach, making me roll my eyes in frustration. Last week, my beloved *Merc'* window was shot out and it took three days to get it back from the police. There's just so much violence in this part of the city. It was never ever this bad when I was younger, but then, the youth's these days are much braver...

I eye the group of boys shouting at each other to my right. They clock me but I quickly turn away.

See nothing, know nothing.

Just a few more yards to my car, so I walk faster. Most people know me around here, but I'm not taking any chances.

The conversation between them becomes increasingly heated and then I jump from the sound of a gunshot. My wing mirror falls to the ground and panic sets in. I run towards the back of my car for cover as the shots continue, but before I can get down behind it, an arm is suddenly around my side, pulling me down to the asphalt.

"Ahhh." I wince in pain. *Fuck*, my head.

"Shhh. Don't. Move," the voice warns. It's authoritative, forceful and not to be ignored.

The arm around my waist tightens and I nod my head in acknowledgement before squeezing my eyes together as the shouting gets louder. There's a scuffle and then an ominous flick of a knife.

My life so far plays before me. It's been good. If I die now, I can be happy with what I've achieved.

The shots continue and then the man beside me reaches for something in his jacket. My head throbs; I'm sure blood is running down my face. A shot fires above me, making me jump.

"Go after him, then!" The voice shouts before muttering something about being idiots, but I barely hear him because my heart is drumming violently in my ears. I'm clinging to his arm; not even knowing who this man is but being thankful as fuck for him.

Footsteps scatter as the group runs away and the arm around my waist disappears.

"Please," I beg.

"It's alright, they're gone."

I open my eyes and specks of bright, white light flood my vision. The body moves from beside me and stands while I sit up and touch my head. Its dark, but with the orange glow of the street lights, I can see the blood on my fingers.

Shit.

Two hands effortlessly lift me up from behind and I gasp in surprise. Lightheaded, I stumble back to rest against my car. I see my bag on the ground and reach for it but I'm beaten to it. The man collects up my things, and I cringe as he even picks up my Tampax...

Oh God.

I breathe deeply as the world spins. I lean over and try to breathe steadily but I'm so overwhelmed, I can't think straight, not even to inhale.

"Here," the man says as he offers me my bag.

I shakily take it. "Thanks."

"You're bleeding," he tells me.

"I know."

"Is this your car?"

I nod. I almost died. *I almost fucking died.* Bursting into tears, I cry, and not quietly but with big, heaving sobs. I cover my face... I think back to when I used to get mixed up in my brother's fights and it makes my breath catch. He almost died so many times... I take a deep breath and let out a sob; *calm down.* I really need to get home.

I wipe my face with the back of my hand and suddenly feel embarrassed when I realise the man is still standing in front of me. "Sorry," I croak.

"No, I'm sorry."

I look up, blinking through teary eyes before my eyes settle on his. He's standing out of the light so I can only just make out dark skin and dark eyes. He's staring at me and I'm staring back just as hard. I can't see the exact shade of his eyes but for a moment, I lose myself in them. *Fuck...* his features are so strong, so masculine and my stomach flutters. I pull my eyes away from him, embarrassed, again.

"Thanks, for helping me," I mutter after finding my sense and rummaging through my bag to pull out my car keys.

"Don't thank me. That was my fault."

I nod my head knowingly but don't look at him. So he's one of *them*. Obviously. Looking like that, how could he not be?

"Are you good to drive?" His fingers touch my face and he wipes some blood away from just above my brow.

It hurts and I flinch. "Yes."

"Alright," I think he says.

"Stay out of trouble," I mutter before I turn away and pick up my broken wing mirror and get into my car. *Stay out of trouble? What the hell?*

I watch him in my rear view before I pull off and see him still standing there. Maybe I should have offered him a lift?

No Layla, fuck that, he almost got you killed... but he also saved my life. I shake my head and concentrate on the road ahead. I need to get my ass home.

***

AFTER TWENTY MINUTES, I reach my flat. I've thought about that guy the entire drive home. Wow, he was *nice*. His body was built, and those features...

I go straight to the bathroom to check my face. I've grazed the right side of my forehead and it looks quite bad. I get some cotton wool and warm water and clean it up. It stings like hell and after I've picked out the gravel, I apply some antiseptic cream to it. I've never had any cuts or grazes on my face and I'm getting angry the more I look at it. I tie my long hair into a high ponytail and remove the makeup from my face. My caramel skin looks unusually pale and I begin to feel dizzy again.

After a few more deep breaths, I get my Pyjamas ready and moisturise my skin, giving special attention to my right side. I have a tattoo from the side of my breast, down my waist and thigh to just above my knee. I designed it myself; it's a dire Wolf under a dream catcher with caves and scenery around it. It's black and shade mostly, with colour only in the wolf's eyes and the beads on the dream catcher. Marco did my ink because he's the only one I trust to do it to my standards.

I climb into bed and wonder how I'm going to explain this massive graze on my head to the girls tomorrow? They are not gonna let it go unmentioned so I better think of a story fast, and a good one at that.

I study the ceiling in a daydream. *That man though...* His eyes were soul-catching and although he didn't say much, his voice... *Ugh...* I groan and roll over and hurt my cut up head, forgetting about it already.

Fuck my life.

CHAPTER 2

I TRY TO COVER the scabbed parts of my head when I do my makeup ready to meet the girls for lunch. My studio's open today but I don't work weekends. I work hard enough during the week so I refuse to spend my weekends there as well.

The makeup approach doesn't work, so I try to work around it, failing hopelessly. Giving up, I get dressed in a skirt and a crop top; my usual 'out of work' dress code. Why have a tattoo if you aren't going to show it off? I wear some flats to match and call a taxi to take me to Central.

I'm meeting my girls, Kelly, Kara and Eve. We regularly meet up on Saturday's for lunch and then have drinks. I haven't been under anyone for a few weeks, too, so I intend on getting someone back to mine tonight.

After I pay the driver and get out, I walk up the busy path to the traffic lights. A black range with tinted windows stops and lets me cross. I thank myself mentally for wearing this outfit and throw my hand up as thanks before I run over to Carlos Bar and Grill. I love this place. They do the best barbecue in London and we've been coming here for years because of it.

"Layla!" Eve shouts from the bar as I walk in. I see their faces drop as I walk towards them.

"What the fuck happened to your *face?*" Kelly asks bluntly when I reach them.

"Let me get a drink first, please," I gush, giving them all a quick kiss on the cheek. "Hennessey and coke, stat," I tell George, our barman. He always looks after us when we come in.

"Damn girl, it's on the house," he says with a grimace while eyeing my wound. I thank him and pull up a stool in-between the girls. They all stare at me, wide-eyed.

"That looks horrible!" Eve says.

"So, what happened?" Kara asks.

George hands me my drink and I down a large mouthful. What am I actually gonna tell them? I can't tell them what really happened... My brother ran a crew. *I'm not a snitch.*

"On my way back to the car after work last night, some guys were fighting in the car park and I kinda got knocked over."

"What the fuck!" They say, almost in unison.

"I know. They were really apologetic afterwards, though, and one guy helped me."
I can't stop the smile that spreads across my lips as I remember that specimen of a man...

"He was hot, wasn't he?" Kelly smirks. They know me well.

"Girl, you have no idea. It was dark, obviously, so I didn't get the perfect look, but what I did see of him..." I drift... His beautiful eyes... I've always been a sucker for beautiful eyes—and he had them.

"Girl, if you could see your face!"

I snap out of my daydream as the sound of the gunshots ring in my ears. I shudder. "It was seriously scary though, they were really going at it. I cried and everything. *So embarrassing.*"

"Hey!" Kara says gently, reaching over Kelly and holding my hand. "It's alright, I would have shit myself."

If only she knew the half of it. "Thanks, babe."

My older brother basically grew up in a gang but he managed to get out and now lives in Australia with his wife and three kids. I always got caught up in his fights because we were only a year apart in age, but last night was the closest I'd personally ever been to being shot.

"So do you think I'll be able to get a pity fuck tonight?" I ask them. I'm hopeful.

"With that head? Hell yes." Eve laughs.

I love these girls, they can always make me feel better. We've known each other since school and been best mates for over nine years. We've travelled together, lived together, laughed, cried. There's not a lot we haven't done together.

"Okay, so I have some news," Kelly says abruptly, "Josh and I are getting married!"

"*What?* Where's the-"

"Here!" She pulls out a ring from her bag and slips it on before proudly showing us all. The rock is huge. No surprise there as Josh works in business.

"Oh my God, Babe, I'm so happy for you!" I suddenly feel emotional. Wow, good for them.

We all take turns to hug her. I know she's wanted this for so long. They've been together for six years.

"Do you think twenty-eight is too young to get married?" She bites her bottom lip and fiddles with the ends of her long, blonde hair.

I scoff. "Hell no! And you and Josh? You two were made for each other!"

"Agreed!" Kara adds excitedly.

"Now we really have to go all out tonight, girls. George?" I call out, waving my hand, "bottle of Moet when you can, please."

"Of course, ladies, what are you celebrating?" He looks intrigued.

"Kelly and Josh are getting married!" I tell him excitedly. I can't believe one of us is finally getting ball-and-chained.

***

I'M SURE WE'VE HIT every bar in Central now. It's four in the morning and we're so hammered I'm surprised we even know our names. I've made out with so many guys tonight but I'm *way* too drunk to fuck, so I decide it's best to go home alone.

We call it a night and after getting food at Chen's Chinese, we walk up the high street to the taxi rank. I hug my Chicken and Vegetables for heat while we wait in line for a car to arrive; we always share a taxi and get the driver to do drops. Kara, Eve, Kelly and then Me.

"Congratulations, Beautiful." I hug Kelly tightly as we pull up outside her house.

"Thank you. Call you tomorrow?"

"Okay, Babe."

She gets out and I tell the driver to wait until I see she's inside. We always do this and I have to text the other girls so they know I'm inside safely when I get home. I live the furthest away from Central so I'm always the last to get dropped.

I rest my head back on the seat and close my eyes. I'm exhausted, and drunk. I feel like I've only just closed my eyes and the driver is tapping my leg to tell me we've arrived. I pay him and get out. He drives away and I reach inside my bag for my keys and phone.

Car lights shine on the side of my face so I turn and get blinded by the light. I squint and make out a black Range, with tinted windows? The driver's door opens—but I ain't waiting to see who gets out. I run up the steps to my house and the security light switches on, blinding me further. I'm so drunk, fuck...

"Find the hole, find the hole..." I mutter anxiously as I try to put the key in the lock the right way around. I hear heavy boots coming up the steps behind me. I panic and drop my keys. They fall behind me and down the step.

Shit.

I'm so dead now...

"You need some help gettin' it in?"

I gape at the door when I hear his voice. I turn around and it's the guy from last night, only this time, I'm getting a really good look at him. I can feel my body literally going into meltdown as I take him in. He picks up my keys and then his eyes pin me to the spot. They really are stunning, a deep brown like his skin, and those lips... *I would like to kiss them...*

He stands beside me and slides the correct key in the lock... the right way around... the first time. He looks down at me before he turns the key and pops it open. I stare back at him in silence, feeling suddenly sober along with something else. His eyes flicker to my head and it knocks me out of my trance.

"We need to talk, Layla."

"Talk? About... wait, how do you know my name?"

"Can we go in?"

I look over to the car he got out of and notice it's still running. There must be someone else inside.

"Layla, I know you've been drinkin', but this will only take a minute," he speaks again... he says my name, again... he has an accent... London badman, mixed with something else.

"Okay." He saved my life, I guess I can give him a minute. If he wanted me dead then surely I would be by now, or maybe that's why he's here?

I hesitate but soon push the door open to step inside and pull my keys from the lock. Holding it open, I invite him in. My heart seems to malfunction every time I look into those eyes, so I avoid eye contact. I smell his cologne as he passes me; damn, he smells good.

Closing the door, I watch him as he walks through to my living room and switches on the floor lamp like he owns the place. *Authoritative...* He's built... *he must lift weights.* I wonder what his body is like under that black jacket and jeans.

He runs a hand over his faded hair and I sense that maybe he's bothered about something. I bet he thinks I'm gonna talk. I drop my bag, Chinese and keys on the hallway table and then walk into the living room. My shoes tap on the wood flooring and he turns around to face me just as I sit on the arm of the sofa and kick them off.

"You don't talk much," he comments.

You make me fucking quiet, that's why. Ugh, *I am so drunk.* I shrug my shoulders and glance up at him quickly before looking over to the window. "I'm not a snitch if that's what you're worried about." I cross my arms defensively.

"I didn't say you were."

"So why you here?" I feel his eyes on me but I can't look at him. Those eyes are a hazard.

He doesn't reply, so I reluctantly turn to face him. I see his eyes fixed to my thigh piece. The look on his face makes me feel naked so I cough to draw his attention away from it. His eyes find mine but I have to look away again. I shake my head while I walk over to the window. Why the hell is he making me feel like this, in my own damn house, too!

"I need to know what you saw last night."

I flinch as I remember it. Those gunshots... "I didn't see anything."

"Layla, I need to know what you saw, no bullshit."

I bite my lip. He actually wants to know? Why?

"You can tell me, I just need to know."

I sigh heavily. "I saw a group of boys fighting... then gunshots, you came along and then..." My mind wanders off to last night and the way he held me... I chance a look at him and he's staring. My whole body tingles; I think I'm losing it.

"And then?" he prompts.

"Uhmm, I heard more shots and that's it." I shrug and run the edge of my curtain through my fingers and thumb.

"Could you recognise anyone if you had to?"

Is that a trick question? Does he want me to say no? Besides, the only one I remember is him... "No," I turn to face him. "No one."

He nods thoughtfully but then his eyes wander again. I can see he likes me, his eyes feel like hands, they're all over my body. He stalks towards me and my heart races again; he does crazy things to my breathing... I step back and lean against the wall, I feel drawn to him but I also feel like I need to get away.

I suck in a breath when he holds my jaw in his hand and turns my face to inspect it.

His jaw clenches. "You had this looked at?"

"No," I answer quietly.

His brow furrows and his gaze repeatedly switches from my eyes to my wound. He's standing so close to me I can't take it. The way he smells is calling to my body and I know my breaths have turned shallow but I can't help it, his whole demeanour turns me on.

"Put some cream on that," he says as if it's an order and then turns and walks away.

He slams the door behind him and I watch through the window as he gets in the car and drives away. I let out a breath I hadn't realised I was holding and close my eyes. I feel so aroused... but I don't even know him.

CHAPTER 3

I SPEND SATURDAY with my Mum. She's a good distraction from that guy, especially because she wouldn't stop banging on about my mash-up head.

Long.

I can't get that guy out my fucking mind. I hardly slept because of thinking about him. I wonder if I'll see him again. It's probably not a good idea, he's like forbidden fruit. It's probably what Eve felt like, looking at that damn Apple.

After dinner, I came back to mine. I'm meant to be going out tonight, but I'm so tired. I also keep thinking about those gunshots and feel mentally drained. I run a hot bath and listen to some Afro Beats while I soak in the scorching hot water. I scroll through Facebook and reply to some work emails. My thoughts constantly go back to him; I imagine his hands on my skin, his lips on my lips... I press my thighs together... ugh, I groan... I seriously need to get over it. This is ridiculous, I don't even know him!

My phone vibrates in my hand. It's Eve.

"Hey," I answer, sitting more upright in the water.

"Hey, you ready?"

"Eve, I told you earlier, I'm tired."

"Sleep when you're dead, ain't that your motto?"

"You can't use my sayings against me!"

"I just did. You have twenty minutes, I'm on my way."

"Eve!" She cuts me off and I sigh.

I quickly get dressed in one of my custom made dresses that cuts out most of the right side of my body. It's rose gold, covered in sequins and shows my thigh and a bit of my hip. It clings to my curves and sits just below my ass. It's slutty but if I'm going out tonight I need to pull, anything to take my mind off of that guy.

I slip on a pair of black stilettos and pack my essentials into a black, matching clutch bag; gloss, mirror, phone, gum and a miniature bottle of Diamond spray. I manage to touch up my makeup just before I hear beeping outside and then I quickly join Eve in the back of the taxi.

"*Damn, girl*, are we on the pull tonight?"

"Hell yes. My plan for tonight is less drink and more man." I hope my face doesn't ruin my plans.

She laughs but agrees. Eve is always a good wing woman. She's beautiful, with long, blonde hair, blue eyes, legs that go on for miles and perfect full lips. She's got that sultry, dirty look about her that men go crazy for. She's single, too, so we can really have some fun.

"I thought we could go to Elite tonight, work put us on the guest list," she says, reapplying some gloss to her lips. She works for one of the most successful advertising companies in London. Her job comes with lots of perks which she always shares with us girls.

"Sounds perfect. Seriously, Eve, you know that guy I told you about yesterday?"

"Yeah?" She smiles knowingly.

"I can't stop thinking about him. I think I need to fuck him out my system."

She laughs. "Oh, bless you, Babe. Don't worry, We'll get you a nice rich guy to bed tonight and all will be forgotten."

"I hope so."

We reach Elite and walk straight past the queue of people and up to the door.

"Eve," the bouncer says with the guest list in hand.

"Hey, Dave. I should be on the list," Eve replies, flirting with him.

"Even if you weren't, I'd let you in."

"Aww thanks, Hun."

"No problem," he says, letting us pass. "You ladies have a good night."

"Thanks," we say in unison before we go inside. We head straight to the bar and order some shots. I remind her of my main goal for tonight but she still orders a bottle of champagne from the bar. She carries the bottle and I bring the glasses to a corner booth at the back of the club with a full view of the dance floor.

I stand by the table and dance while I enjoy a glass of Dom. The alcohol starts to seep into my blood and when *Akube* by Dotman comes on, I down my drink and drag Eve to the dance floor.

"I love this song!" I shout at her.

"Me too!"

We dance together for half the song and then two guys approach us. I think they're brothers, but I can't be sure. They're cute, so when one of them starts dancing with Eve, I let the other dance with me. He stands behind me and rests his hands on my hips as we move to the music.

"I love your outfit," he says in my ear.

"Thanks!" I roll my hips against him and he's instantly hard. Feels like a decent size too. Eve looks at me and I discretely wink at her.

"I'm Jason," he says confidently before spinning me around. He pulls me against him and we continue dancing. He flicks his messy, blonde hair from his face and gives me a devilish smile. He has pretty blue eyes that twinkle when the strobe lights hit them.

"I'm Layla," I reply, wrapping my arms around his neck. We dance for a little while longer before the boys pull us over to the bar to buy us drinks.

Jason makes small talk while we wait to be served. He's twenty-nine and works in finance with his brother, Greg. He asks me how I hurt my head and I give him some fuckry story about falling over. He kisses my cheek and smiles sympathetically at me. He's sweet.

We get our drinks and return to our booth with the boys. I see that Eve's mouth is getting on really well with Greg's. Jason looks at me as he puts his glass down. I know he wants to mimic what his brother's doing with my friend and kiss me. I watch him intently as he leans towards me. He slips his hand around my neck and pulls me in. I bite my lip...

"Layla."

My eyes dart up and past Jason to see *him*. He's wearing a black shirt that's open at the top few buttons. It fucks with my mind; he's showing just enough of his silky dark skin to make me wonder if he tastes as good as he looks. The arms of his shirt are almost ripping from the strain of the muscles underneath and *oh, wait... oh god...* he's inked. I can see it peeking out from just under where his shirt sleeve ends. I follow his shirt buttons down his body to his dark blue jeans but blink rapidly as I realise how long I've been checking him out and quickly return my eyes to his.

"Uh, what are you doing here?" I ask sounding rude as hell. I can feel Jason's eyes on me, too, but I ignore him.

"I need a word," he says casually, taking my hand and pulling me over Jason and out of the booth.

"Layla?" Eve shouts, taking a breath from Greg's mouth.

"I'll be right back, okay?" I tell her, showing her one finger.

"Keep an eye on her friend," he tells the guy dressed in black beside him.

"Got it." He nods at me, but I just blink, confused.

My 'so-called-hero' confidently holds my hand and leads me through the crowd of people on the dance floor, right to the other side of the club. Two bouncers either side of a pair black double doors hold them open as we approach. We go up two flights of stairs in silence and through another set of guarded double doors and into the VIP area of the club. I question myself on why I'm going with him, but deep down I know the answer.

He releases my hand and wraps his arm around my back and side so he's touching me. I feel like my body's on fire as his skin connects with mine. I look up at him but he doesn't seem affected at all.

At the bar, he requests a bottle of Amaretto Ciroc to be sent to his table and then leads me over to a private corner booth at the rear of the VIP. I slide in and he follows close behind me. My heart is pounding so hard right now. He sits close and his cologne teases my senses. I bite my lip as he turns to face me and when my eyes find his, they take my breath away.

He's *so* gorgeous...

He leans towards me. "That can't be your man 'cus you wouldn't have let me take you away from him like that."

I shake my head in response, unable to speak but not knowing if he was asking a question or making a statement. My head is so fucked.

"I don't think you're always this quiet." He runs his fingers along the bare skin on my thigh. I feel hot just from his touch and have to take several deep breaths to steady my breathing.

The barman appears at our table. "Mister Brandon, your Ciroc, Sir. Should I pour?"

"No, thank you," he replies but doesn't look away from me.

I hear the barman put the glasses and bottle on the table. "Sir."

So his last name is Brandon?

"That's not my real name. Why don't you ask me what my name is?" He finally looks away from me and pours us both a drink. I feel like I'm being pulled into a dark hole. He's mysterious but comes across as dangerous at the same time. He hands me a glass and gives me an expectant glare.

"What's your name?" I try to sound confident but don't know if I succeed. I sip my drink. I need to get a grip, *God*! He's just a man.

"Neymar, but I go by Jackson."

Hmmm, Neymar. I like that. "How do you know my name?"

"I know things. He smiles and it disarms me.

I nod and take a longer sip of my drink, I don't think downing it would make a good impression. "Who's the boy?" he asks, putting his glass on the table and turning his attention back to me.

"Jason. I met him tonight," I say quickly, feeling uncomfortable as if I'm being judged. I take another sip of my drink.

"Were you gonna fuck him?"

It takes all my mouth strength not to spray my drink all over this table. I finally manage to swallow hard and compose myself. I calmly put down my glass and cross my arms before narrowing my eyes at him. "And that's your business because?" I ask harshly. *Who the fuck does this man think he is?*

He laughs for a second but quickly stops. He slips a hand around my waist and finds the opening of my dress. I have to look away because I feel like his eyes—not his hand, are invading my personal space.

"Don't act shy. I've been watching you all night and you ain't looked it."

He's right; I'm not shy, but he makes me. I sigh with frustration. What the fuck does he want from me? I turn back to face him. "If this is about–"

"It's not, and don't mention that again." It's a warning and my stomach turns at his tone. He takes his hand away from my waist and drinks from his glass. I feel like my mother's just told me off and suddenly feel really self-conscious. "Have you been putting cream on that?" he asks, glancing at my grazed head.

"Yes, thank you," I answer defensively. "Look, I should go," I tell him and stand. I need to get out of here. Maybe I could find Jason and still get some much-needed sex as I'm clearly not getting any dick here.

"Sit." He slips a hand around my thigh and pulls me back down onto the seat. I blush hard and slap his hand away. Seriously, as much as he's pissing me off, he is still turning me on, *badly*. I pull down my dress and try and stretch it to cover my skin. I don't want him to touch me; it feels too good.

His fingers find my chin and he lifts my face so I'm forced to look at him. "Do I make you nervous, Layla?" He leans towards me so his lips are only a few inches from mine.

Those eyes... "Yes," I snap, "and I don't like it."

"I think you do."

"Well, you're wrong."

"I'm never wrong."

I scoff and roll my eyes. "Sure."

His face moves to my neck and goosebumps ripple across my skin. "I bet you want me so bad right now." The words spill from his mouth with no shame whatsoever. He kisses me behind my ear and I close my eyes until I feel him moving away. I can't deal with this shit, he's too much...

"What do you want from me?" I sound desperate, and I am. He's getting to me in a serious way and I'm struggling to keep myself together.

"What makes you think I want something from you?"

"Well, if you don't, can you please stop fucking with me!"

There's goes that smile again... *ugh, I give up.* I'm pissing myself off because I have no control over this situation.

"Do you want me to fuck with you?" His expression is serious, all humour, gone.

"Boss."

"Layla! What the fuck?"

Neymar turns away from me and I am slightly relieved that I don't have to answer his last question.

"Eve, sorry, I was just–"

"Nice to meet you, Eve," Neymar says as he stands up to shake her hand.

"Oh my God, is this?" she gushes, shaking his hand but staring wide-eyed at me.

"Is this, who?" he asks, annoyingly intrigued.

I nod and roll my eyes. Shit.

"You're the guy who helped her? When those boys were fighting and knocked her over," she explains and I mentally congratulate myself for not telling her the truth.

"Is that what she told you?" He sounds surprised.

"Yeah, you're such a gentleman," she gushes and I have to hold in a snort. If you only heard what he was just saying to me.

He smirks and I watch his friend break into a smile, too. I have a strong feeling that these guys are extremely far from gentlemanly. "I wouldn't say that. It was the least I could do, please, sit with us."

"I can't, I just wanted to see if Layla was ready to go but I can-"

"Yeah, I'm ready," I tell her hastily, standing up and downing my drink.

She frowns. "Are you sure?"

I wish we had some kind of code for these situations. I try to give her a stare on the sly but I know Neymar sees me. I can't think straight right now, all I know is that I need to get as far away from him as possible.

"Do you girls need a ride?" he offers.

"Yes," Eve answers.

"No," I say. God, please no.

"Layla, it's gonna be a nightmare getting a taxi now. Why can't he drive us? He helped you before, it's not like he's gonna kill you now."

If only you knew that he's been killing me since I fucking met him. "Okay," I answer reluctantly and pinch the bridge of my nose with my fingers. When I look back at them I notice Neymar staring at me. I frown and he looks away, making me sigh. "Let's go, then."

The car journey is awkward. I'm usually a chatterbox when I've been drinking but Neymar is killing my mood. Eve is doing enough talking for us all, but for once, I'm glad. She's unabashedly hitting on Neymar's friend or whoever the hell he is. He has flawless, dark skin like Neymar, and is completely her type. She wants to like the good guys but really, she loves the bad.

"So, you got a girlfriend, big boy?" she finally asks as her interrogation comes to a close.

"Yeah, I do."

"Ugh, of course, you do. Well, she's a lucky girl."

I smile at her response. She's so blunt, I love her. I feel eyes on me and I look at Neymar beside me. "How long you known each other?" he asks, seemingly interested.

"Since secondary school."

He nods his head and looks back out of the window so I do the same.

"So, am I seeing you tomorrow or you going to your dad's?" Eve asks me as we turn into her road.

"I've got some sketches to do for Monday and I need to go see dad, yeah."

"Okay, that's cool. I need to visit mum anyway. I guess I'll see you next weekend then?"

"Of course." We pull up outside her house and she leans in the back to kiss me on the cheek.

"Nice to meet you, Jackson and..." she stalls... "...nameless."

"Jay, my names Jay," he replies and I'm sure he rolls his eyes.

"Nice to meet you, Jay. See you later, babe," she says to me.

"Night, Hun."

I watch as she climbs her steps but then Jay starts to pull off.

"Wait! I never leave her until I know she's inside." I get anxious as my routine is almost disturbed.

"No problem." He pulls up the handbrake and waits.

I lean over to Neymar's side and watch her find her keys and get inside. She waves and I wave back before she closes the door. I catch Neymar's gaze as I sit back over my side of the car but quickly face forward. "We're good to go," I tell Jay and he pulls off.

I'm assuming I don't have to tell him where to go, I'm sure this is the same car that he came to mine in last night and...

"Were you following me yesterday?" I ask, turning to face him. "Outside the grill, when I crossed the road, that was you!"

"It was."

I frown. "Why?"

"I needed to talk to you, but I couldn't get you on your own."

I nod slowly. "What is *with* you?"

He laughs and reaches for my hand. I leave it where it is and he squeezes it. "Nothing."

"Nothing, right. Well, I don't have time to play games with you, Neymar." I pull my hand away and cross my arms. I stare out the window and feel relief when I realise were literally minutes from my house.

"Are you hungry?" he asks softly and I exhale deeply. Hot and cold should be his first and last names. I am hungry... I usually grab Chinese after a night out but I'm not telling him that.

"No, I'm good."

"You sure? Jay can take you somewhere."

Jay, right, the driver... it wouldn't be him, would it? "I'm sure."

I unbuckle my seatbelt as Jay pulls up outside mine. "Thanks for the lift home, Jay."

"No problem, Layla."

Neymar gets out onto the pavement and motions for me to come out his side, so rolling my eyes, I scoot over and get out of the car. He shuts the door and follows me up to my door. *Is he gonna try to kiss me?* My heart races as he leans in next to me while I'm finding my keys. I find the right one quickly this time and slip it into the lock.

"Layla?"

"What, Neymar?" I ask impatiently as I push the door open. I put my foot inside to stop it from closing and turn to look at him.

"Thanks for not telling your friend what really went down the other night."

I sigh and nod at him. Of course, he's just happy I'm keeping my mouth shut. "I told you, I'm not a snitch. Goodnight, Jackson," I say and walk inside.

"Goodnight, Layla," he says before he turns to walk down the steps. I slam the door and throw my stuff on the side table before sitting in my living room. What the hell is his problem? He cock-blocks me, speaks in code and then leaves me hanging? I seriously need to forget about him, he's going to be bad for me no matter how I look at it and I have no intention of feeling like this for any longer than I have already.

CHAPTER 4

I SPEND SUNDAY morning with my dad and then head home to do some sketches ready for work on Monday. I'm doing a back piece tomorrow of a lioness and cubs on a woman's back which I'm really excited about doing.

After dinner, I reply to some work emails and then decide to call Eve. She'll only send me abusive texts if I don't.

"Hey, babe," she answers.

"Hey, Hun, you okay?"

"I'm fine but how are *you?*"

"Frustrated. I would have slept with that Jason if Neymar hadn't shown up."

"I know, right. He was gutted when you left."

"Really?"

"Yeah, come on, do you blame him? You looked amazing in that dress, actually fuck that dress, you always look amazing."

"Well, I clearly didn't look amazing enough because Neymar didn't even try to kiss me."

"What?"

"I know. He teased me and then didn't even try anything."

"So he cock-blocked you for nothing?"

"Yep. Apparently, he'd been watching us all night and then seemed to have planned his attack at the crucial moment."

"Wow, that's harsh. It doesn't make sense, though... why block a cock from you if he didn't want to give you his?"

"Fuck knows but the guy is seriously getting under my skin, Eve, I need to get over him... he's no good, I can feel it. Ever since I met him, he's all I think about, it's not healthy."

"He is fit as fuck, though, Layla, I don't blame you for crushing."

Crushing? More like half obsessed... "I know, God, I just need to get laid to get over him. This is why I wanted to get laid last night. I need to fuck him out my system."

"A man like Neymar would ruin you for anyone else, especially if the sex is bangin'. It's probably a good idea not to taste what you can't keep."

Her words stab at me but I quickly brush it off. "I know, you're right."

"Don't worry, we'll get you some cocky on Friday night."

"Please."

"Alright, Babe. Speak to you in the week."

"Okay, Hun. Speak soon."

"Bye."

"Bye." I hang up and lie back on my sofa. What am I gonna do? I can't even think straight...

I HEAR MY ALARM and get up straight away. My first appointment is at ten this morning and it's the lioness and her cubs. I love when I get to have a creative input in someone's tattoo. I've designed three styles for her so I'm hoping she likes one of them. I have a favourite but I'm not going to try to force it on her. I'm just grateful for being the one that gets to ink it.

I sit in traffic and my mind starts to drift to Neymar. I turn up my stereo to try and drown out my thoughts but it's useless. He's literally driving me crazy and he hasn't even done anything.

I park the car and instantly remember Friday night. I shudder at the memory and walk quickly to the studio. I relax once inside my haven... maybe I should move the shop? The fighting around here is getting way too much.

"Who's early this morning?" Johnny says, smiling at me.

I spin on the spot and take a bow. "Moi."

"Wait, hold up, what happened to your face?"

Shit, I forgot about that. "I fell over on Saturday night. Heals," I say, giving him a knowing look.

"Damn girl, that looks nasty."

"I know. I'm fine though."

"Good. Coffee?"

"Yes actually, I'd love one. I also need a favour?"

"Sure. What's up?"

Some idiot knocked off my wing mirror, don't suppose you could take it to get it fixed for me?"

"Course, there's not much for me to do today. Let me get caught up and I'll come grab the keys from you."

"Thanks, Hun."

I hang up my coat by the door and make my way over to my station. I say hello to Maverick and he glares up at me with his iron in hand.

"Eyes down," I say as I walk past him towards Marco. He's rummaging through a box in his draw as I approach. Marco is covered in tattoos, most of them done by me.

We ink each other because we are very particular about how we like our tats to look. He sighs deeply and I cough to make him aware of my presence.

He turns around and blinks hard. "What the hell is with your *face*?"

"Shhh, customer," I scorn him and point behind me to Maverick.

He stands and takes a closer look. He towers over me and I roll my eyes at his reaction.

"Sorry. What happened?"

"I fell over on the weekend. Didn't handle my drink very well."

I can tell he doesn't believe me. "That's not like you."

"I know. I'm fine though, looks worse than it is. Anyway, what about you? Everything okay?"

His jaw tenses and I know it's not. "Emily, she's pregnant."

"What?"

"Yep."

"Oh dear." He's only been with her a few months and he was only telling me the other week he was thinking about ending it with her. "What happened?"

"Fuck knows, I'm always careful. I don't want a baby, Layla." He looks defeated.

"Look, don't worry, okay? Everything happens for a reason. Just make sure that even if you don't stay with her, you're there for that baby, you hear me?"

"I know." He sighs. "I just, I'm pissed off with myself."

"Of course you are, but a baby is a blessing."

"I don't want my kid growing up without me, but I don't want to be unhappy for the rest of my life either."

"You don't have to be with her to be there for the baby."

"Don't I?" He gives me a knowing look.

"Not all women are the same, Marco, and besides, I won't let that happen. I'll fight with you if it comes to that, you know I will."

He hugs me and I frown into his chest.

"How do you do that?"

"Do what?" I ask curiously.

He releases me. "Make everything better?"

I shrug. "Do I? Fuck knows," I mutter. I had no idea I did that. I wish I could make everything better for myself.

"Yeah, always."

"Well, I'm glad I can be of some use." I check the clock on the wall. "I gotta get set up, but don't worry, okay?"

I get to my bench and Johnny appears straight after. "Sorry, just quickly, we had some guy in yesterday requesting you ink him this week."

"Did you tell him I'm fully booked?" I ask while getting my inks ready. This is nothing new.

"I did but he offered to pay double if you could fit him in."

"And what did you say?"

"I said that I'd speak to you about it but I know you're really busy. He said he'd be back today to speak to you personally."

"Johnny! You know I'm chocka today, right? I doubt I'll even get a chance to pee."

"I'm sorry but he's not really someone you say no to, if you know what I mean."

I hear the door and look behind him. It's my ten o'clock. "Okay, I'll deal with it Johnny, just get me my coffee, alright." I stand up and wave Tori over.

When she reaches me, she starts gushing. "I am so excited. I have waited so long for this!"

"Aww, bless you."

"Honestly, like I told you before, I'm like your biggest fan. I've been so excited to see the final sketches."

"Well, I have them here on the table if you want to have a look." I walk over to my desk and spread out the three sketches I did yesterday. Three designs of a lioness surrounded by her cubs.

"Layla." She shakes her head and covers her mouth. "They are amazing. How am I meant to choose one?"

I laugh, and then explain the concept of each design and the placement of each one on her back.

"I love them all, but this one is perfect," she says as she points to the one on the left. A lioness roaring surrounded by four sleeping cubs. The lioness symbolises her, and the four cubs are her children. Not my favourite, but still amazing.

"Great choice. Are you ready?"

"I have a question but I'm not sure if you'll be able to do it"

"Go on."

"I know I said I wanted it done in colour, but the way you've drawn it in black and white, I wonder if you could do it like that instead?"

I smile because I think it would look better without colour, too. "Yeah, course I can."

"Brilliant, thank you. Now, I'm ready."

"Okay, then I need you to remove your top, there's a towel there for you to cover your front with and then lie face down on the bench, okay? You can just unhook your bra."

"No problem."

Tori tells me about herself while I'm inking her. She's here for a three-hour session but will need two or three more to complete the back piece. She tells me about her husband leaving her after she fell pregnant with her fourth child, so she's raised them on her own while going to college and studying to be a teacher. I think it's the perfect profession for her to go into, she's inspirational.

"Do you need a break?" I ask her as she hisses when I work on her lower back.

"How long left to go?" she asks, painfully.

That's a yes.

I check the time on the clock on the wall. "Another half-hour."

"Would you mind if I went for a quick cigarette?" she asks politely and I smirk.

"Of course not. Give me two seconds." I finish the fade on the bottom of the mane and then wipe her skin. "I'll need to wrap you up quick but you can go out back to smoke if you want so you don't have to get dressed again."

"Yes, thank you."

I quickly wrap her and help her up. She stands and gently wraps the towel around herself before grabbing a smoke from her bag. I show her out the back to the little garden and head back inside. I make my way to Johnny at the desk and check my schedule for the rest of the day. My next appointment is at one-thirty.

"You doing a lunch run when you take my car to get fixed?" I'm blatantly hinting.

He rolls his eyes. "I can."

"*Please.* I'd love some BBQ. Means you get to drive her for longer. No rush in getting back either, we'll be good here." I raise an eyebrow at him.

His eyes sparkle with excitement. "Deal."

I know he loves driving my car. "You are so easily convinced," I laugh as I hear the door go.

"Shit, it's him," Johnny mutters under his breath.

I turn around and my smile is wiped from my face. I roll my eyes...

"Layla."

"Jackson." I cross my arms.

"You know him?" Johnny whispers.

"Kinda," I mutter before I return my attention to Neymar. God, those eyes look as beautiful as ever. *Shit.* "I heard you came in yesterday?"

"I did."

"I'm with a customer now, but I'm free in half-hour if you wanna come back?"

He smiles and my body starts shutting down again...

"I'll wait." He takes a seat on the leather sofa by the window. I bite the inside of my lip and sigh.

When I turn around, Johnny's eyes are almost popping out of his head.

"Lunch and car," I snap, feeling irritable, and then I walk back to my station just as Tori is coming back in from outside. I check the time and then work on her for another half hour before wiping her clean and wrapping her up.

"Here are the after-care instructions. Any problems, call us, okay?"

"Got it. Thank you so much, it's looking amazing already," she gushes.

"It's my pleasure. I enjoyed designing it."

"See you in two weeks?"

"I'll be here."

I follow her to the front desk so she can pay before leaving. I try and calm my nerves as I return to my station to clean it down. Neymar wants me to ink him? Is he fucking serious? I groan inwardly as I realise I can't delay speaking to him any longer so I go over to him. He looks up.

"Do you wanna come through to the back?"

"Sure."

He gets up and follows me to the back of the shop. I avoid eye contact with the boys because I don't want to deal with their reactions right now. I take him into the office and shut the door.

I lean against my desk and he stands a few steps away, by the door. I feel more comfortable knowing he's out of arm's length.

I sigh. "You want me to ink you?"

His eyes light up. "Yeah."

"Why?"

"Because you're the best."

I hide my smile at that, but it's true. "Seriously? Do you really think that's a good idea?"

"Why wouldn't it be?"

Why would it be, more like. "Where do you want it?" I ask, but instantly regret my choice of words.

He flashes me a devilish grin and I roll my eyes. He quickly removes his t-shirt. "What are you doing?" I gasp as my eyes are burnt from the gorgeous specimen before me.

"Showing you where I want it."

I try not to stare at his Adonis-like body, but I fail miserably. He's closed the gap and grabbed my hand. "I want it from here..." he says softly, placing my hand on the left side of his chest... "...up to here," he continues, sliding my hand up his hard body, up to the base of his neck. My eyes lock with his and he looks deeply into me. I watch his lips part and I'm sure his breathing changes. His skin is so soft, I want to touch him everywhere...

I regain my senses and snatch my hand away. I have to inhale sharply. Why is he tormenting me like this? He knows I like him, and I'm sure he likes me, too, so why the mind games?

I walk around my desk and sit down, desperate to get some distance between us. I mindlessly look through my schedule for a distraction.

I need to say no.

"I'm booked up for months, Johnny told you that, right?"

"I'll pay you double."

I look up at him and try to focus on his face. "Please, put your clothes on, *God*."

He laughs but pulls his shirt back on.

I scowl at him. "It's not a matter of how much you're going to pay me, it's a matter of when I can do it. I mean, what do you even want done?"

"I want you to design me something. Something dark but with an angel in it."

I sigh but I'm intrigued by his choice of design. "I can sketch out something, fine. But I can't fit you in. I work ten 'til seven most days, and I don't work weekends."

"I'll pay you triple and you can do me after seven, or on a Saturday. I'll make it worth your while. Don't think of it as work."

"You're paying me, it's work," I snap back.

"I won't pay you, then."

I give him my trademark glare and he laughs. He's really sexy when he smiles... *God, help me.*

"So, after seven, or Saturdays, your choice." He looks hopeful and I piss myself off because I know I'm going to cave.

"How soon do you want it doing?"

"Soon as."

I try not to roll my eyes, so I stare down at my desk instead. Why am I even doing this? Maybe because he saved my life and I owe him? *I really need to stop using that as an excuse.*

"I'll sketch some ideas tonight, then you can tell me what you think of the designs," I tell him in defeat. I'm way too nice, that's my fucking problem.

His eyes alight with triumph and I hate him for it. "Take my number, then you can call me when you're done."

"Fine." He gives me his number while I type it into my phone. I stand to see him out and he looks at me expectantly. "What?"

"Ain't you gonna give me yours?"

"No. You'll get it when I call you, won't you?"

He rolls his eyes. "Fine."

"Right, it's been nice, but I'm going to be late for my next customer if you don't get out."

"Always so eager to see the back of me," he replies and I'm unsure if it's a joke or if he's being serious. Either way, he has no idea.

I open the door for him and walk him out. I see my next customer waiting and feel annoyed that Neymar has made me run late.

"You'll bell me, then, yeah?" he asks as he reaches the door.

"Yep."

He looks over my body and makes me feel naked again before he leaves. How the hell does someone do that with their eyes? I turn and the boys are glaring. I ignore them and luckily have to work back-to-back for the rest of the day to catch up, so they don't get a chance to question me.

WHEN I GET HOME, I have a quick bath and get comfortable in a set of grey, two-piece loungewear. It's basically knitted leggings and a cropped top. I warm up the barbecue that I didn't get a chance to eat at lunch and get out my sketch pad and play some *Sia*. Her music always helps me get to the dark side; her voice is just so intense. I sit at my desk in the living room and adjust my lamp, giving me the best light.

So... *Something dark, but with an angel incorporated...*

I draw an enchanted angel with long black hair, crying softly into a pool of dark, swirling liquid. I make it flow down into a waterfall of skull pebbles. I look at the sketch when I'm done and wonder if this is how I feel about Neymar.

I draw another two sketches, one without the sculls and instead I make the water flow into a cave, then another, with fire and the angel burning. He never said if he wanted colour or shade, but it doesn't matter because these can be done either way. I don't tattoo from stencil; I always ink straight onto the skin with my sketches to guide me. I glance at my phone and debate calling him now... I check the time, it's midnight. He might not even be awake.

I finally decide to call but put my number on private first. If he doesn't answer then he won't ever know it was me.

"Jackson," he answers on the second ring. He sounds annoyed.

My stomach tightens at the sound of his voice. "Neymar."

"Layla?"

My breath catches. *Fuck.* I swear, there is so much meant in the way he says my name.

"Private number?"

"I wasn't sure if you'd be awake," I reply softly.

"I don't sleep much."

"Me either."

"Is that so?"

"Um, yeah... anyways, I've finished your sketches."

"I'll come now."

"You don't have to, we can do it tomorrow."

"If you're tired we can leave it. Otherwise, I can be there in ten."

"Uhh..." The nerves kick in and I second guess my decision to call him.

"I'm coming over," he says before hanging up. I slowly put my phone down on the desk before going to check my face in the mirror. My forehead is healing, but it's slow going. *Ugh...* I wipe away the smudged makeup from under my eyes and then make my way to the kitchen to make a tea.

The door knocks while I'm pouring hot water into my cup. I leave it to stew and walk to the door. I see his silhouette through the smoked glass and take a deep breath. This man is so unsettling.

I open the door and he smiles as he sees me. "Layla."

"Jackson." I smirk and he rolls his eyes before he steps inside. I notice his hair, he's had it re-faded and it looks good on him.

"If you hadn't withheld your number, I would've known it was you."

"You don't have my number so you wouldn't have known," I throw back at him. I close the door and walk back into the kitchen. I feel his eyes on my bare mid-drift while I remove the tea bag from my cup.

"I would have known cus I don't give that number out."

"Hmm." I nod. Is that so? So I'm special enough to have his private number. Aren't I lucky? "You want a drink?" I offer.

"Coffee, if you have it."

"White or black?"

"Black."

"Sugar?"

"One."

I make his coffee and then hand it to him before finishing up making my tea. He sips his drink and I cringe. "I've literally just made that. How can you drink it so hot?"

He smiles. "Habit."

Ugh, those lips though. I shake my head before walking back into the living room and putting my tea down on the desk. Neymar stands beside me while I spread out the sketches across my desk.

"You didn't really give me much to go on, so I don't know if any of these will be suitable," I tell him, feeling more nervous than ever. I'm so confident in my work but he makes me feel so self-conscious and nervous about even that. I watch him as he silently looks over the drawings. I want to say something to end the silence... I feel so uncomfortable...

"This one, but I want that Wolf you have on your thigh put into it somewhere." He hands me the picture of the Angel crying into the pool – with the cave.

"The Wolf on my thigh?" I can't hide my surprise. When has he even had a chance to really see that?

"Your tattoo is the sexiest thing I've ever seen." His voice is unusually silky, soft. He walks behind me to my right side and unravels me with such an intense look that it ignites a flame inside me. "Can I see it? All of it?"

My heart races at his sudden change in demeanour. *Hot and cold.* I stupidly say yes and put down my tea and the sketch. I lift my cropped top up to under my breasts and show him the dream catcher and how it links to the landscape that creeps down my waist and hip. I watch him closely and see how his eyes scald my skin. It feels so forbidden showing him this, it's been a while since anyone admired it like he is – I don't even know if anyone ever has.

I hesitate before I show him the next part. I feel nervous about showing him my thigh piece because I'm not wearing any underwear. After a moment, I look away... here goes...

I grab my crotch and then hook my thumb into my leggings, turning away from him slightly before sliding them down enough for him to see the Wolf part on my thigh.

"Fuck." His tone is harsh, making me jump. He reaches for my skin and runs his fingers over the wolf's face. My ass is blatantly on show and I feel flushed as hell because of it. My heartbeat drums loudly in my ears while he touches me so softly, so intimately. I do want him to touch me, but really I want so much more than just this. He's literally driving me insane with wanting him.

He snatches his hand away and sighs deeply, as if pained. I pull up my bottoms and decide to save him by ending the awkwardness. "So, I *can* incorporate the Wolf, I designed it myself anyway so that's not a problem."

He stays silent so I put the sketches into a pile and then pick up my tea and drink some.

"I can't drag you into my world, Layla."

I frown as I swallow a mouthful of tea. *He can't drag me into his world?*

"I can't want someone like you because you'll get hurt." He closes the gap between us and slides his hand around my bare waist. "I want you, but I can't, I'm sorry."

His hand tightens on my skin. I nod in response, but I don't really know what he means. What do I say to that? I want you too, but I understand? Understand what? I know he's gonna hurt me, Eve was right. Men like him don't come into your life without causing irreparable damage.

I don't need that.

I step back. "After I do this, this tattoo, stay away from me, okay?"

"Layla–"

"Please, don't. Ever since I met you you've been fucking up my head. I can't take it. If you want the tattoo done, that's fine, but after that, just please don't. Please."

I can see he's hurt. He doesn't hide it well at all. He nods before leaving and my chest strangely aches to see him unhappy, but I need to protect myself.

"Drop by the studio tomorrow and I'll show you the new design," I call out to him. I think it's best we're not left alone with each other.

"Yeah."

I walk into the kitchen and hear the door shut as he leaves. Tears sting my eyes but I don't even know why. I don't even know him, but he's had such an impact on me. What the hell is it about him that makes me feel this way; I just don't get it.

I tip my tea down the sink and return to my desk. As I turn to a fresh page in my sketch pad, I hear his car pull away. I sigh heavily and replay his words in my head. *His world?* I know he's into some street shit already, that was obvious the night we met.

Ugh, fuck this! I'm not going to make excuses for him. I'm just gonna do this sketch, ink him, and then move the hell on.

CHAPTER 5

I BRING NEYMAR'S SKETCH into work with me and find myself clock watching all day.

He doesn't come in.

My mind feels like it's constantly in two different places at once.

I finish up with my last customer and after he pays me, I lock the door behind him. I sterilise my station and put my kit away, but then I suddenly feel angry at the fact that I can't get Neymar out of my fucking head.

What is wrong with me?

I slam my kit around, and after the anger, all I feel is frustration. I'm becoming emotionally unstable. This is exactly the reason why I just do one night stands. I turn out the lights in the shop, shrug on my coat and grab my bag. I look at the time, it's seven thirty. Setting the alarm on the door, I leave and lock the door behind me.

That's how most of my week goes. I don't see Neymar, and I don't contact him. By Friday, I've convinced myself—with some help from the girls, that it's best this way.

And that's why I'm now drunk as fuck in club Ivory, in South London. Kelly went home early, but me, Eve and Kara are chatting away nicely to three hotties at the bar. We decide to take the party home and pile up at the rank to get taxis. I hug the girl's goodbye and make them promise that they'll text me as soon as they get in.

"Blow his mind," Eve whispers before she quickly gets inside her taxi.

"I will," I mouth at her through the glass.

She winks at me and then I feel Cole's hand on my thigh. He kisses my neck and I sigh. I hope I judged his dancing right in the club because I need him to give it to me good.

The next taxi arrives and we quickly get inside. I give the driver my address and Cole moves over in the back to me.

"Your tat is hot as fuck, Leela," he says, running a hand up my thigh.

"It's Layla, and thanks," I say, rolling my eyes. He tries to talk but I kiss him to shut him up. He's a good kisser but my mind wanders to Neymar and I imagine that it's him. He feels up my breasts through the fabric of my dress and I can't help but imagine that they're his hands on me, too.

"You're so hot," he breathes against my mouth. I know I don't really like this guy; I just need to fuck someone to get Neymar out of my system.

We pull up outside my house and Cole pays the driver. He gets out the taxi and I follow behind him. "Which house is yours, babe?" he asks while wrapping an arm around me.

"That one," I tell him, pointing to my house with the white door. I rummage through my bag and quickly find my keys so we can get inside.

I drop my keys and bag on the side. Cole starts kissing my neck and exploring up my skirt but I hold my hands high and quickly message my girls on our WhatsApp chat to tell them I'm home. Their replies come through almost straight away so I drop my phone on the side and focus on Cole.

He kisses me, and I eagerly kiss him back, grabbing his short spiky hair between my fingers. I moan as he catches my bottom lip between his teeth and then slides his hand further up my dress.

Oh god... I so need this... He squeezes my breasts in turn and I moan softly.

"You like that, Baby? Fuck... you have incredible tits," he mumbles against my lips. I kiss him more urgently in response while he reaches inside my thong. I urge him on, desperate for contact, making work of the buttons on his shirt, but abruptly he pulls away because we hear banging on the door.

"Who the fuck is that?" Cole asks harshly, stepping away from me. "I thought you lived alone?"

"I fucking *do* live alone!" I snap, feeling angry at the frustration I feel. Seriously, I've never found it so fucking hard to fuck!

I turn around and step to the door, swinging it open angrily.

"Neymar? What the fuck?"

Neymar, dressed all in black, glares at me before pushing the door and stepping inside like he owns the place. "No, more like *Layla* what the fuck?" He walks past me and I glare back at him. Who the fuck does he think he is?

"It's Leela, actually, and who the fuck are you?" Cole asks, stepping up to him.

Neymar easily towers over him and I slump in defeat.

"Layla, get this clown out of here before someone has to drag him out."

Cole clenches his fists. "Who the fuck-"

I step between them. "Cole, please, I'm sorry but you need to go." I hand him his coat off the floor. "I'll call you, okay?" The last thing I need is a fight in my house.

I push him out the door and close it.

"But you don't have my number!" he shouts through the glass before I hear him calling Neymar a prick as he walks down my stairs and into the street.

I turn to face Neymar with my arms crossed. He looks angry as hell but I am fucking livid! How fucking dare he!

"What the fuck is your *problem?*" I shout at him, outraged. I barge past him and walk into the kitchen.

"What is *my* problem? What the fuck do you think you're doin', bringing some next man back here?"

I spin around and give him a deadly stare. "I'm twenty-eight years old, I can do what the fuck I like! I haven't heard from you all week and the last time I did, you gave me some bullshit excuse about not getting me involved in your shit."

"It wasn't a fucking excuse, Layla. I was being honest with you!"

"You said you were going to leave me alone but yet here you are again, fucking cock-blocking me for the second time!"

He laughs but not for long, it's more of an accident. "I've been working some shit out, you couldn't wait, no?"

"Wait? For what? I met you two weeks ago, Neymar. You've barely touched me! All you've done is turn me on and then leave me frustrated, and then," I scoff, "you've stopped any chance I've had to get laid. You're fucking selfish!" I point my finger at him. "I bet you're okay though, I bet some sket is sorting you out! I have fucking needs, too!" I fling my words at him. I fucking hate him right now.

He looks stunned, regretful even. "Layla-"

"No! I don't wanna hear it." I wave a dismissive hand at him and then walk past him back to the front door. "I want you to get the fuck out and leave me alone." I unlock the door and hold it open.

"You don't mean that." He regards me cautiously but doesn't move from the kitchen door. It infuriates me further.

"I do, Jackson. Seriously, you need to leave."

I'm shaking I'm so mad. How fucking dare he come here like this and stop me hooking up with another guy when he made it crystal clear that he didn't wanna get involved with me.

He finally walks towards me and rubs his head in his hands. Those eyes catch mine and I inhale sharply. He looks at me and I stare back at him with my hand on my hip. My heart is racing from anger but my body is starting to betray me because it still wants him.

Damn it.

My anger quickly sparks again, though, because I know that once he leaves here, I'll be left wanting and I just can't take it.

"What are you waiting for? Leave," I tell him again, but this time I don't really mean it and I think he can tell.

He steps closer to me and I try to stay mad but deep down I just want him to touch me or kiss me or *something.*

He pulls me into his arms and buries his head in the curve of my neck. He kisses my skin and my anger disappears.

And just like that, I want him.

"I'm sorry," he whispers against my skin and I sigh deeply. He slides his hand up my leg, over my tattoo to grab my ass, hiking my dress up to around my waist. I hear him breathe deeper as his hand moves to my inner thighs, leaving a streak of burning fire in their trail. He plants soft kisses along my neck and I have to hold onto his shoulders to steady myself.

Suddenly I'm overwhelmed. *He's touching me... he's actually touching me... Fuck...*

He slides his hand higher until he reaches my thong and then pushes it to the side like he owns what's inside.

"Please," I moan as he slips a finger inside my slit. *Oh, please...*

He groans against my skin when he feels how wet I am and then mumbles something under his breath but I'm too far gone to hear. He snakes his free hand around my waist and backs us up against the door until it closes, then his arm pulls me towards him as his finger finds my sensitive place and strokes it gently. I close my eyes and push my hands up under his t-shirt, feeling his ripped torso and silky soft skin.

He mumbles something again, but my heart is pounding so hard, I can't make out the words.

"Open your legs," I hear and do as I'm told. He shifts his hand lower and pushes two fingers inside me.

"Neymar," I moan, pulling him in. *Fuck... it's too much...*

"Fuck, Layla," he groans before pulling the skin on my neck between his teeth, making my skin throb. He rubs his palm against my clit and my hips instinctively rock against it, desperate for more contact. He quickly gets the hint and presses harder against me, giving me the friction I so badly need.

I gasp his name as he makes me come... hard... *so fucking hard...*

My body is still shuddering when he takes his hand away from me.

I take my hands out from underneath his t-shirt and try to compose myself. Blushing hard, I take my weight off his arm that's around my waist and stand up straight, pulling my skirt down over my hips. He moves his head from my neck and looks down at me.

I can't describe the look on his face. His eyes search mine and I start to feel guilty. What if he was telling the truth earlier? He's such a mystery, I just don't know what to think of him.

"I have to go." He looks torn, and for the first time, I see some genuine emotion on his face.

I decide to not make him feel bad and let him go. "It's okay."

"I'm sorry."

"I'm sorry, too. I didn't mean to upset you."

"I know."

He disappears into the kitchen to wash his hands and then returns to me at the door. "Can you message me a time you're free on Monday so I can look at them new sketches?"

"Yes, I will."

He shocks me by kissing my forehead and then I open the door for him. He steps outside and turns to look at me briefly before walking down the steps. I close the door and sit on my stairs. I can't believe that just happened. I blush with embarrassment. If I was sober there is no way that would have happened. Or would it? I'm so confused, but I do feel better after coming. Guilt washes over me... what about him? I never even offered.

Shit.

CHAPTER 6

I GET TO THE STUDIO EARLY to look through my schedule. I have a break between twelve and one so I tell Johnny not to book me in anything for then and text Neymar a simple message telling him I'm free between that time.

I clock watch all day and then as I sterilise my station after my eleven o'clock appointment, I hear the door. I look over and see him come in. He looks good; wearing dark grey chinos and a grey jacket. I want to smile but memories of Friday night fill my mind.

Oh, God...

I tidy away my things and then walk over and ask him to come into the office. I feel so embarrassed; I can't look him in the eyes.

He closes the office door and I quickly spread out the sketches on my desk. "Here they are," I say, stepping away and letting him take a look. We swap places and once again he's quiet. He turns around to look at me while leaning on the desk but I fix my vision on the pictures. My shame is real.

I hear him sigh. "Is this about Friday?" He stands upright and steps towards me. I nervously play with my hands, desperate for a distraction. "Look at me."

"I can't."

"Why?"

"Because... I feel... embarrassed."

He lifts my chin and his stunning eyes search mine. I feel so exposed when he looks at me like this. "Why?"

I shrug. "Because of what I said, *what we did.*"

"I gave you what you needed, what's there to be embarrassed about?"

That was far from what I needed. I shrug again. "Because... what about you?"

He smiles. "Thanks for your concern, but I'm fine."

My stomach knots. Maybe he does have other girls on standby. "Don't you..." I swallow hard, "...want..."

"You?" He frowns. "Of course I do, but it's not that simple."

I wasn't going to say, me, but his confession is intriguing. "But why?"

"Because with you it's different, and I know once we go there," he shakes his head. "There won't be no goin' back."

I blink hard and try to make sense of what he's saying.

"I'm an all-or-nothing kind of man, Layla, and I can't get you involved in my shit right now."

He never makes sense. I feel like he talks in code most of the time.

"I was bein' real with you when I said what I said. I've been tryin' to work some things out for a while. Change my lifestyle. Meeting you has made me more determined to do that, but I need you to be patient with me," he says as if it's a plea. "And I can't focus if I'm thinkin' about you fuckin' any fool you meet at a club that can't even get your beautiful name right."

He looks at me knowingly and I cringe. *Ugh... Cole.*

"I'm sorry," I whisper.

"No, I'm sorry. You were right. I knew you liked me and I knew what I was doin', but I didn't think about your needs."

"But you don't seem to be affected by me at all."

"It might look that way, but there's nuff you don't know. I can't do what I want with you, not yet."

"How do you always seem to know what I'm doing?"

He drops his hand from my face and returns to the sketches. "I know things."

"Are you following me?"

"I'm not."

Oh shit. "So you're having me followed?"

He sighs. "I want to know you're okay."

"Are you crazy? You don't have to follow me!" I hiss.

"Ain't you noticed there's been no drama 'round these ends since that night?" he says quietly.

I let his words sink in. He's behind that? Oh no, this is worse than I thought... "Neymar, I-"

"I want this one," he says cutting me off and pointing to one of my sketches.

I walk over to my desk and look at the design he's chosen.

"When can you start?"

"I've managed to move my appointments back an hour, so if you can make six o'clock every day this week I can do it then."

"I can do that. Should I come back tonight?"

I nod and watch him as he takes his hands off the desk.

"I'll see you tonight then?"

"Yeah."

I see him out in silence and feel the boys staring at me as I do.

When he's out the door I turn around and see them all looking at me. "Don't even. It's not what you think. I'm just inking him and that's all."

"Make sure," Maverick warns.

I nod but don't say anything.

Why?

IT'S FIVE THIRTY and the boys have just left for the day. I sit at Johnny's desk and look through my schedule. Johnny has done such an amazing job since he's been here, I think it's time I spoke to Marco and Maverick about upping his wages.

My stomach rumbles from hunger so I raid Johnny's snack drawer and eat a bar of *Dairy Milk*. Work has been so busy the last month, I barely get time to go to the loo, let alone eat. I must have lost at least half a stone in weight.

I reply to some work emails and check the Facebook page. I start clock watching again and realise that all I seem to do these days is wish away the time until I get to see Neymar again.

The door goes and I look up and see him. He smiles and this time I smile back. Those lips.... *Oh, God...* He's changed clothes since earlier and is now dressed in all black. Black jeans, black t-shirt, black jacket and black Tims. He walks over to me so I get up.

"So, you ready?" Excitement rushes through me at the thought of inking him.

"Yeah." He raises a curious eyebrow as if it's nothing, but I noticed he didn't have any tattoos on his neck and I know it hurts there.

"Alright."

I walk over to my station and he follows. He stands by my chair and we look awkwardly at each other. He had no problem taking his shirt off before, so why is he hesitating now?

"Don't go mad, okay?" he says cautiously.

"Okay," I reply slowly, wondering what I might go mad about. Does he have scratch marks on him from someone else? Jealousy bubbles inside me. He takes off his shirt and I see a bandage on his upper right chest. "What the fuck is that?" I ask, but deep down, I already know.

"Calm down, it's nothing." He tries to brush it off, but that is *not* nothing.

"Bullshit!" I feel a head-fuck of emotions but mainly anger. I struggle to control it. "When did that happen?" *I bet it was last week.*

"Last week."

I nod knowingly as his disappearance last week becomes clear. Of course, it did. I take a deep breath and pull on my gloves. "Lay down."

I hear him sigh as he walks over to me. He lies back in my chair and I sit on my stool, adjusting it to his height so I can get a good angle on his chest.

So he went and got himself shot, and then he avoided me.

He could have died... it's not that far from his heart...

I bite down on my lip to steady my voice before I speak. "I'm gonna start with the angel at the top, on the base of your neck," I tell him. My words stumble as the anger I felt is replaced with sadness. I've never been able to hide my feelings very well and as my eyes keep wandering to that bandage, I struggle not to burst into tears with my worry for him.

"It's okay, I'm good, okay?" he says to reassure me.

I nod but turn away from him to compose myself. I find the steriliser and take a few deep breaths. I turn back to him but don't make eye contact. I feel his eyes watching me, though, while I wipe his skin down in the area I'll be working on.

"Colour or not?" I ask, forcing myself into work mode.

"What do you think will look best?"

"On your skin? I think no colour."

"No colour then."

I set up my machine and lay out the sketch on the movable table beside me. I take a good look at the image of the angel and get comfortable next to him. He looks at me and I look at him quickly before I press my foot to the pedal, and then my full concentration is on the ink.

I know these hours will go quickly, but I'm still looking forward to spending time with him every day this week, even if it won't be for long. I don't really know much about him at all, I wonder if I'd be overstepping if I asked him some questions.

As I start the outline of the angel's face on the base of his neck, I feel him flinch and I smile. "Everyone is so tough until they sit in my chair."

"It doesn't hurt."

"Of course it doesn't."

I feel him looking at me but I stay focused. I'm a perfectionist when it comes to my work and no matter how much I like him, I'm not gonna let him ruin that for me.

"Tell me about yourself," he says as I feel him flinch again.

"What do you want to know?"

"Anything."

"Well, I graduated from art school when I was twenty-two. I have an older brother who's twenty-nine. I've been tattooing since I was fifteen, and I have three best friends, Eve, Kara and Kelly."

"You started inking at fifteen?"

"Yeah, Indian ink. I'm not really proud of that, but that's where I started."

"Savage."

"I know." *Ugh, they are not my proudest moments...*

"You think you'll get any more ink?"

"Yeah, I want my side piece extended, and I've always wanted a sleeve done, but I'm not sure how, yet."

"I love your ink. When I saw that wolf on your leg at your house that night... shiiiit, I thought it was so, fucking, sexy."

39

I glance up at him and he's staring at the ceiling. I smile to myself as I wipe down his skin and decide to ask him some questions.

"Do you have any siblings?" I ask as I press my iron harder to his skin.

"Mmm, I did."

I release my pedal and pull up from his skin for a moment. "Shit, I'm sorry." *Fuck... wrong question.*

"It's okay... life." He looks at me with those beautiful eyes and my heart leaps. I nod before getting back to work and wonder what the story behind that is.

"Next question," he says. I'm surprised he's giving me permission to ask more.

I decide on lighter questions. "Favourite colour?"

"Black."

"That's not really a colour."

"It is to me."

I roll my eyes. I could argue all day the reasons why it's not, but I'll let it go. "Favourite food?"

"Hmmm, soup."

"Soup?"

"Yeah, there's a place in North London that does the best fish soup."

"I never would have guessed that you'd be a soup kinda person but okay, what about favourite animal?"

"Wolves, now."

I smirk but keep focused on my work. I wipe his skin and then lightly shade around the angel's eyes. "Why?"

"Since I saw your tattoo, I can't get those eyes out my mind."

"I love how they follow you."

"They do."

I smile and look up at him as I briefly lift the iron. "What do you do to relax?"

"I don't. I don't have time to relax. But maybe soon."

His work. When my brother was in a gang, he never switched off. I feel bad for the life that he lives.

I couldn't go back to worrying about someone like that...

I feel the back of his hand rub against my side. "What are you thinking about?"

Straddling you, right on this table. What? No... I was thinking the complete opposite. "Just about life, y'know?"

He lets out a tormented sigh. "Yeah."

I finish the angel's hair and then hang up my machine. I wipe his skin and look at his bandage again. It kills my mood.

This man...

I wrap him up and then give him a copy of my care instructions when he sits up. "I know you're a busy man but take care of it, okay? The end result will be so much better if you do." I reach into my drawer and take out some barrier cream and hand it to him. "Use this."

He takes it from me and slips it into his pocket.

"You can pay me when I finish it, alright? I know you're good for it."

"I am." He smiles and pulls his shirt on. When he gets up, I sterilise my equipment and start cleaning my kit. I feel him watching me as I work and suddenly feel nervous. When he pulls up his zip, I remember how those fingers felt between my thighs and sigh deeply.

"I'll walk you to your car," he offers as I finish putting my things away.

"Okay."

I lock up the studio and we walk in silence to the car park. When I reach my car, I turn to face him. My eyes are drawn to his lips but I blush hard and look away. He hasn't kissed me yet and I can't stop thinking about how his mouth would taste.

He smiles knowingly. "Same time tomorrow?"

"I'll be here," I say nonchalantly, but I struggle to hide my disappointment as he opens my door for me. I get inside and he closes it before turning and walking away. I sigh with frustration before starting the engine. I'm starting to wonder what it will take to get him to handle me more. I'm all for the gentleman type, but I know Neymar isn't one and I just want him to put it on me.

Hard.

CHAPTER 7

TOMORROW IS HERE, and he's in my chair again. Today, I'm doing the angel's body; she'll be kneeling by the side of the pool of liquid by the end of the session. Neymar is even more quiet than usual and hasn't said more than a few words to me since I started half an hour ago. I feel his eyes constantly on me, though, and it repeatedly makes my heart race. The more time we spend together, the more I feel things for him – like, I crave to be around him. I know I'm playing a dangerous game, but I can't seem to stop myself.

"You wanna get something to eat after this?" he asks out of the blue.

I take a quick look at him, surprised by his question. "Yeah, sure."

He goes quiet again but my mind goes into overdrive. He's asked me out on a date? Or maybe he's just asked me because he's making me work late and feels bad. Nah, I doubt he'd feel bad over that...

I finish most of the angel and then wrap him up. I watch as he pulls his shirt on and admire the way his muscles flex under that incredibly smooth skin.

Fuck.

I start thinking of all the things I would like to do to that body.

My God...

I roll my eyes and groan in frustration, a bit too loudly because he hears me.

"What's wrong?" he asks while stepping beside me.

"You." I look up at him and he wraps his arms around my waist.

"You smell good," he says softly and kisses my forehead.

This isn't helping... *he* smells good, and he feels so strong.

I want to be under him.

"You smell good, too." I pull myself away from him, I need distance. He might be able to resist me, but I want so much more than what he's giving out.

"Layla–"

"Let's eat, I'm starving."

I think he gets my point. He nods his head before turning away and pulling on his jacket. I lock up and see that the range is parked at the kerb. Jay greets me warmly when I get inside.

"We're going Lolas," Neymar tells him.

"Ah, seen. You taking Layla to try the soup?"

"That's the one."

"I have high expectations for this soup," I say as my stomach growls. I really am hungry.

"I wouldn't like to disappoint you."

I raise a brow at him and he smirks. He always leaves me disappointed, so I'm hoping he doesn't with this.

We reach the restaurant and Neymar leads me inside. We sit at the back at a table for two and when the waitress comes, Neymar orders us both calamari for starters and the fish soup for main. He asks if I want a drink but I stick to lemonade. He's still being quiet so I decide to ask him some questions.

"So, do you like it, so far?" I ask him, tipping my head at his chest.

"I love it."

His gaze is intense and I blush for some reason before looking away. "Good."

"How many more sessions you think I need?"

I trace the rim of my glass with my finger. "I'll be finished the angel tomorrow and most likely get some of the pool done. The Wolf will take more time, but, if you don't have to rush off at seven then I can work a bit longer and try finish it Friday evening."

"You ain't got to rush."

I look back up at him. "I never rush my work."

The calamari arrives and it's delicious. I have very high hopes for the soup now. I've had fish soup before, my mum cooks it for me often, but I don't usually like to order things like that when I go out to eat because most of the time, it's disappointing.

"Do you always go out drinking at the weekend?" Neymar asks after a long lull of comfortable silence.

"Usually, but now Kelly is getting married and Kara is seeing someone, we might calm down a bit. I know Eve likes someone... I don't know what will happen." I shrug. We're all getting older now so I guess we'll start settling down.

"Do you want kids?" he asks abruptly and I blink in surprise.

"Yeah, I do. Do you?"

"If my life changed, then I would." He looks deep in thought. I wish I could read his mind.

"Neyma-"

"Let me take these empty plates for you guys. Your soup is almost ready," the waiter says as he appears at the table. I smile and lean back to let him take my plate.

Neymar looks at me as the waiter leaves us. I decide to tell him how I actually feel. Might as well, nothing else is working.

"I really like you, but you're so closed. I feel like, even though I do like you, I don't really know you at all."

"That's fair. I've not really told you anything about myself but I don't have much to be proud of." Maybe he doesn't think I can handle his lifestyle. Maybe if I told him about my brother he would open up to me?

"You helped me that night and you didn't even know me."

His eyes bore into mine and I bite my lip. I want to know what goes on in that mind of his.

"I got you into that situation, it's the least I could do."

I don't get to reply because our soup arrives. I blow some on the spoon and then taste it. Wow, it's amazing. The fish is so soft and the flavour of the broth is intense.

"You can admit it, it's good, isn't it?" He smirks and I roll my eyes.

"Yeah, it's amazing."

"Well, I've never heard you use that word before so I'm guessing you don't just throw it around."

"I don't." I think about sex with him and then wonder if that would be amazing. Just thinking about his body covering mine makes me all hot and flustered. I blush at my thoughts.

"I bet it will be."

I look up from my soup and frown. "What will be?"

He swallows a mouthful of soup and licks his soft lips. Oh *God...* my heart just stopped.

"Sometimes, I can't read you, but other times..." He shakes his head and smiles, "...I know *exactly* what you're thinking."

I narrow my eyes. "Is that so?"

"It is."

"Hmmm." I look back down and exhale. Maybe I'm playing this all wrong. I think I need to start pushing his buttons a bit more so he gives me what I want.

On the way back to the studio, I think of a plan to test Neymar's rock-hard resolve. He's been so controlled and I've been so nervous, I think it's time to turn the tables. When I get home I text my dressmaker and ask her to come over on Saturday so I can discuss some new designs with her.

I need to blow Neymar's mind.

I need sex.

IT'S WEDNESDAY, and when I dressed for work this morning, I made sure to look my best. I'm wearing a blue cropped top and low rise leggings with slits up the side. My total midsection is exposed and my leggings allow my Wolf tattoo to peak out through the slashes.

The boys don't seem phased by my choice of clothing at all, I've worn much more revealing outfits to work before, and even if they did say anything, I would just say I was trying to promote my work. Simple.

I hear the door go at a quarter to six, just as I'm tactically hanging a sketch of my work up on the wall. I look behind me and see Neymar standing by the door. His eyes are on my body and I smile inside. This is exactly the reaction I wanted. I ignore him and finish straightening the frame before getting down off the step ladder. I fold it up and lean it against the wall, making sure to give him a good view of my ass as I do.

"You ready for me?" he asks, making my stomach tighten. I know that's not what he means, but I decide to play him at his own game.

"I've been ready," I reply and turn to face him.

He strides over to me and once he's by my chair he pulls his shirt over his head. His bandage is gone and only the stitches are visible. I look over his body with no shame, still sexy as hell. I imagine it all over me and inhale sharply.

"You good?" he asks sarcastically. I scorn him. He's clearly much better at this game than me. *Come on girl, be strong.*

"I'm amazing." I shrug and pat my chair to motion him to lie down.

He narrows his eyes but I don't let it phase me. He lies down and I wipe his skin, admiring the work I've done so far and comparing it to the other tattoos on his body.

"You're looking after it well. I'm impressed."

"I thought I better do what I was told." He smirks and it makes me feel things.

"You should."

"Yes, boss," he replies with a chuckle and I'm drawn to his lips again. I wanna suck those lips.

I get set up and adjust my stool so I'm a bit higher today. I get started on finishing the angel so that she's kneeling, now. I feel his eyes on me, like usual, and as I start bringing the pool of liquid into the tattoo, I bite my lip as if I'm concentrating. I hear him sigh and I know he's feeling something.

I lick my bottom lip after I release it with my teeth and I feel him shift on the bench. I keep my gaze fixed firmly on his skin but inside I'm smiling so hard. Not so tough now, are we? I wonder if he's imagining my lips on his cock? I've been told many times that I have blowy lips.

Neymar asks me about my day and I sense he's trying to take his mind off my actions. I tell him about the ink I've done today and then I part my lips and exhale softly.

"Why are you doing this to me?" he mutters under his breath. I lift my machine from his skin and fix my eyes on his.

"Doing what?" I tilt my head and look at his lips again... It's only a kiss, but I want him to give me one so damn bad.

He grabs my wrist and guides it over to my table to hang up my machine. He doesn't take his eyes off mine as he sits up, swivels around and puts his feet on the floor. My heart races in anticipation and this time when my lips part it's because I'm desperately trying to suck more air into my lungs.

He leans forward and curls his hand around the back of my neck. I release my foot from the pedal so the humming of the machine stops.

"Is this what you want?" he whispers before he leans in so close to me that his lips are just millimetres from mine. I can feel his hot breath on my mouth and close my eyes. He's so close... *oh God...* He leans forward so his mouth only just touches mine. I gasp at how soft his lips feel and then suddenly they are fully on mine.

Oh... fuck.

I part my lips and suck. My desire overwhelms me and I bite him, needing more. I hear him groan and then his lips press firmly against mine. My hands find the back of his neck and I run my fingertips over just where his hairline stops before pulling him closer.

He opens his mouth and I don't hold back. I tilt my head and devour him. His lips are just as soft as I'd imagined, and he tastes so fucking good. He strokes his tongue against mine and I moan. His free hand finds my waist and he pulls me to stand. I step between his legs and he holds me against his hard body. Our kiss rapidly becomes more urgent and I feel myself becoming lost in the moment as I press my body against his. He groans and the sound makes me shiver. *Oh God,* he's such an amazing kisser.

"Fuck," he groans and breaks away. I'm panting hard and as I step back from him, I can feel the arousal between my legs.

What have I done?

His stare is intense and I have to look away. I turn around and put my hands on my thighs to take a minute. I wanted to kiss him so badly but now that I have, I feel like I've just made the biggest mistake of my life. Eve's words ring loudly in my ears...

He'll ruin you...

I'm ruined so bad.

"Layla..." he says softly. "That..."

I turn round. "Was amazing?" *Please don't say it shouldn't have happened...*

He shakes his head and sighs. "Yeah." But he doesn't look so sure.

"Look, I know, we shouldn't have done that..." *But God, it was so...*

"I know." He groans in frustration. "This is why, this is why I told you. Now I just want more. Fuck!"

"I'm sorry," I whisper. I wound him up and now look what I've done.

"It's not you who should be sorry. It's me. Me, and my fucked up life."

"It's okay. I understand. My brother..." I start, swallowing hard "...he held a crew in London for years before he got out. I remember what it was like for him... *for all of us*."

He looks surprised. "Your brother?"

"Yeah, he managed to get out, but it took him years..."

"So you *know* why I can't get you mixed up in this shit!"

The door goes and we both look to see Jay standing there. He looks at Neymar and shakes his head. Neymar turns to face me and gets up off the bench.

"I have to go."

I can see by the look on Jay's face that something has happened, but I'm not gonna ask any questions.

"Wait," I tell him, quickly wiping down his skin and wrapping him up. "There. Now, you can go."

He pulls on his t-shirt and grabs his coat. "I'll call you, okay?" He looks hesitant.

I nod. "Sure."

He gives me a look then he leaves with Jay.

My head spins. That kiss... I replay it over and over as I clean down my station and feel the effects of it in my thong, every time I move.

Damn.

CHAPTER 8

THURSDAY.

I finish my last appointment at six but there's no sign of Neymar. I clean down my bench and hear my phone vibrating on the side.

It's him. "Hello?"

"Layla. I'm gonna have to cancel today. Something's come up."

How cliché. Play it cool... "That's okay, I could do with an early night."

"See you tomorrow?"

"Sure."

He hangs up and I feel disappointed. Maybe I scared him off yesterday.

Shit.

Well, that backfired, didn't it... I groan as I put my kit away. What am I doing? Neymar's going to be the death of me. I need to just leave it alone.

KELLY TEXT ME on my way home and asked me to meet her at the grill. After getting changed into a skirt and a backless halter-neck top, I slip on a black jacket and then jump in a taxi to go meet her. She's sitting at the bar when I walk in, so I quickly make my way over to her.

I kiss her cheek. "Hey, babe, you okay?"

I slip off my jacket and hang it on my stool. Something is off, she looks nervous. She plays with her blonde hair and can't seem to look me in the eye.

"Yeah, thanks for coming." She slides a glass of Rosé wine across the bar to me and I give her a suspicious look.

"What's wrong?"

She sighs. "I'm pregnant."

"What?"

She nods as her confession sinks in. She's pregnant. Wow. "When did you find out?" I ask while sitting down and taking a sip of wine.

"Just before I called you."

"Does Josh know?"

"No."

"Why not, babe? I mean, I'm honoured that you called me, but he's the one you should have told first."

"He always said he didn't want kids until he was thirty. I don't know what happened, I never miss my pill, Babe." She looks distraught. I put down my wine glass and give her a hug.

"Josh loves you. You know that. He will be happy."

"But what if he's not. I don't want to lose him."

I pull away. "You're gonna keep the baby?"

"Of course I am."

"Then what will be, will be. You must be pregnant for a reason, Hun."

That sounds very familiar.

"I'm so scared," she says quietly.

I squeeze her hand, trying to reassure her. "Of course you are. It's a life-changing situation. I'd offer to be with you when you tell him but I'm sure he'd be pissed that you told me before him."

"Hey, Layla," George greets me from behind the bar.

"Hey George, you good?"

"Yes, thanks."

He smiles before walking away to serve someone, so I turn my attention back to Kelly. I hold her other hand in mine and she looks at me with tears in her eyes. "Babe, this is meant to be happy news, something you've always wanted. He always said he wanted kids, you're getting married and look how good he is with your niece and nephew."

She nods. "I know."

"I can't imagine him being anything *but* happy. Yeah, I know it's happened earlier than he planned, but you can't really plan a baby anyways."

"I know, I know, I just don't know how to tell him."

"Cook him one of this favourite meals, then tell him. Or take him out for dinner if you're that worried. But honestly, this stress isn't good for you or the baby so you need to tell him, soon." Wow, it feels so strange saying that. I can't help but smile, my best friend is having a baby.

She wipes away a stray tear. "Why are you smiling?"

"Because, I'm so happy for you! You and Josh are like family, this is such amazing news."

"Thanks." She smiles but still looks unsure.

"I won't tell anyone you told me first, alright. Just forget you told me."

She nods and wipes away another tear. "Thank you, Layla. You know you're the first person I go to with stuff."

"And you know I will always keep your secrets."

"I know."

"Have you eaten? I'm so hungry."

"Yeah, I have, and I should probably get home. I told Josh I was only popping out."

"No worries, Hun. Get back and tell him the good news. Text me later and let me know how it went, okay?"

I watch her take a deep breath. "I will." She picks up her bag and gives me a hug. "I love you."

"I love you, too."

"Do you want a lift home?"

"No, I'm good. I'm gonna grab some barbecue before heading home."

"Alright, I'll text you later, then."

I nod and I watch her walk out.

"All alone?" George asks appearing out of nowhere.

"Looks like it. Can I get some brisket and ribs to go, please?"

"Sure. About ten minutes"

"No problem, I'll have another wine while I wait."

"Coming right up."

I pay for my food and wine, then scroll through my Facebook while I wait. As I finish my drink, George reappears with my food box in a white, plastic bag.

"I am *so* looking forward to this," I tell him as he hands it to me.

"Enjoy!"

"Thanks, George, see you Friday?"

"You bet."

I leave the grill and walk up the unusually quiet high-street towards the taxi rank. I'm almost there as a group of boys walk towards me. I move to the side of the pavement and squeeze past them almost dropping my food.

"Oi, you," I hear one of them call but I carry on walking.

I feel someone grab my shoulder and I turn around quickly.

"I'm talking to you," the boy says. He can't be older than twenty, *if* that. He's dressed all in black and has a sword tattoo on the side of his face.

Shit work. Tacky, too.

"Me?"

"Uh, yeah you!" He mimics my surprise and the other boys laugh as they surround me.

"You're that fucking sket from the other day!"

I panic as his tone becomes harsher. "I don't know what you're talking about," I answer quickly and then try to walk away.

He quickly grabs my face and squeezes it hard. I try to struggle out of his grip but he applies more pressure. "From the car park."

Oh shit...

"I don't know what you're talking about. Get off me!" I shout and feel relieved as people start to stop and ask what's going on.

"You best not say anything, whore," he says and then leans towards me. "Or you're fucking dead, you get me?" he whispers menacingly. "And me and my boys will rape you first."

I cringe at his words and feel sick to my core. My breathing escalates from my panic and I quickly try to think of a way to get out of this.

"Oi, get off her!" I hear a woman shout and he turns away from me. I jerk my head from his hand and step back from him. The rest of his boys block me from getting past and tears well in my eyes.

"Mind your own business, grandma," he laughs before turning back to face me.

"Look, I don't know what you're-" I hear the sound of a slap and then the pain that spreads across my face is excruciating. I clutch my cheek as a sob escapes.

"Oi, you little cunts, get away from her," I hear a man shout and the group starts to move away.

"Take that as a warning," the boy says before telling his friends to come.

"Are you alright, darlin'?" A tall man with glasses asks me, touching my arm.

I nod. "I'm fine," I whisper, trying not to cry.

"Do you want me to call the police?" There's probably CCTV-"

I shake my head. "No, please, I'm fine. I just need to get a taxi, I just need to get home."

"Alright, darlin', let me walk you to the rank, yeah?"

I thank him and we walk the last few yards up to the taxi rank. I thank the man again before I get in the car and once the driver pulls off I start to cry. My face stings so bad.

"You alright, love?" the driver asks sincerely.

"Yeah, sorry, I'm, okay," I stutter as I clutch my face. It hurts so much... *he was so angry...*

"Where you going, sweetheart?"

I tell him my address and then try to stop crying but I can't. I cry all the way home and then when I go to pay the driver, he only charges me a half fare, clearly feeling sorry for me.

Once inside, I feel relieved. *I'm home, thank God, I'm home.*

I drop my bag on the side and then carry my food to the kitchen and put it straight in the fridge, feeling more sick than hungry. I open my freezer to get some ice and after knocking a few blocks out of the tray, wrap them in a tea towel.

I walk back to my hallway and look in the mirror. "Shit." I cover my mouth with my hand in shock. How on earth am I ever going to cover *this* up? Worry sets in and tears fall again. My cheek is turning a deep shade of purple and even though he slapped the side of my face, under my left eye is swollen and is bruising, too.

I gently press the cloth against my face and hiss from the pain. I slam my hand down on the side table. My fucking face! *Twice, in two weeks!*

I tremble as I remember what he said to me... *'me and my boys will rape you first.'* Oh God, he was so mad. I'm always on that street as well.

I have to stay away...

I make my way upstairs, and after I climb into bed, I hold the ice on my face until it melts and then cry myself to sleep.

CHAPTER 9

I'M APPLYING MAKEUP before work, trying to blend the foundation to cover my face. I don't usually wear foundation, so I'm struggling... a lot. When the girls and me lived together at Uni, they always used to hook me up.

I could use them right now.

The swelling on my face has gone down a lot since last night but you can still clearly notice it. My eye is mostly the problem. I wish I wasn't the boss because then I could call in sick. My customers wait months to see me and I haven't got the heart to cancel their appointments. I'm definitely gonna cancel on Neymar, though. I can't see him looking like this, and in a way, this is *his* fault.

Fuck sake!

I spread the foundation over my bruised cheek and decide to go for a smoky eye to try and hide the swelling around it.

Once I'm done I'm quite impressed. Apart from some visible swelling, I've actually done a good job. Now to get to work. I decide on a grey hoody so I can hide my face when I'm out of the shop. I don't want one of Neymar's spies noticing my face either. Of all the times they weren't fucking watching though...

I walk into the studio and everyone is busy. *Thank the stars!*

I make it to my station just as Johnny finds me. I face away from him and rummage through a drawer while he talks to me about today's appointments.

"What are you looking for?" he finally asks.

I sit up and look at him. "Nothing, what's up?"

"Layla..." he gasps, "...what's wrong with your face?"

Ugh... I guess not good enough.

I stare at him and he gets the hint.

"Are you okay?" he asks concerned.

I nod and fake a smile. "I'm good, okay, just get me my coffee, please?"

"Course." He takes a long look at me before leaving. This is bad. I need to think of a story and quick. If he's noticed then everyone else is going to notice. I decide to text Neymar now, to cancel before I forget. That's the last thing I want or need.

- Can't do tonight, sorry! Rain-check? -

Not a minute after I've put my phone on my desk, it vibrates.

- Kl. -

I sigh with relief. Nice and easy—no questions. He must still be caught up in his mess, which is worrying...

My morning is chocka until two but then not a minute after there are no longer any customers in the studio am I surrounded by three very angry looking men.

"What happened to your face, Layla, tell us," Maverick demands. He crosses his arms while his dark eyes stab at me accusingly. *I really don't need this.* I know Maverick will go mental if I tell him the truth and insist on hunting the boy down that hit me. I love that they are so protective of me, but I really just need to lay low.

"Seriously, guys, I'm completely aware of how bad it looks but I'm fine. I just went out to meet Kelly last night and when I was walking to the rank, some boys were fighting and hit me accidentally." I swallow hard, *my jaw hurts when I talk.*

"What the fuck? Did you call the police?" Johnny questions.

"No, don't be silly," I scoff. "It was an accident."

"Who were you with?" Marco asks.

I cringe. "Kelly had left, I was on my own."

Maverick rolls his eyes but the worry on his face is clear. They look at each other as they start firing questions at me in quick succession.

"Did you ice it?"

"Yes, Marco, of course, I did. I bloody iced it for ages."

"Do you feel alright? Should you even be here?"

The questions annoy me and I snap. "Look, I'm fine, okay? It's all superficial and I don't wanna play the boss card, but please, just drop it, okay?"

They reluctantly agree to leave me alone and none of my customers seem to notice or say anything for the rest of the day which I'm grateful for. I'm pampered by the guys for the rest of the day, with Maverick even staying until I lock the shop at six.

He walks me to my car and I thank him. To be honest, I don't want to be on my own when I'm outside, so I am truly grateful.

"Look, Layla, I know you said drop it, but this doesn't have anything to do with Jackson does it?" Maverick asks as we reach my car.

"No, shit, why would you think that?" I say acting shocked and I think I succeed.

"Because things have been happening to your face since around the time I saw him in the shop. You don't want to get involved with someone like him." He is clearly giving me a warning and I realise there is definitely something between them.

I wonder what it is.

"Look, I'm just inking him, okay? I'm not sleeping with him or anything like that. I mean, I like him, but he hasn't even tried anything." More half-truths... I'm quite the liar these days, so out of character for me.

"He will..." he mumbles. "I've known you for a long time, Layla, I know what you and your mums went through with your brother. The only difference is that your brother would never have hurt you, Jackson on the other hand... he don't care about people Layla, only about getting what he wants. Trust me."

"Maverick, like I said, we aren't involved like that and I'm not looking to get back into that kinda life."

He looks at me and sighs. I know he thinks there's something more going on and he's completely right about my injuries, but I can't tell him that. I know I shouldn't really be protecting Neymar either, but I'm so torn.

He finally lets it go. "Alright. See you Tuesday?"

"Tuesday?"

"Bank holiday Monday?"

"Oh yeah." I'd forgotten. Yep, see you then." I say nonchalantly.

I get home and have a long, hot bath. I gently remove the makeup from my face but my stomach turns because if anything, it looks worse than it did this morning. Panic sets in hard. I don't know what I'm gonna do. Even my neck feels stiff, he really got me good. My eyes well up. I feel so hopeless. The graze on my forehead has only just disappeared, and now this. My face is horrendous and I'm even scared to go out on my own. I already know I'm gonna cancel on the girls tomorrow night because the thought of getting to the grill on my own is making me anxious as fuck.

I HAVEN'T HEARD from Neymar. He must be busy which is good because he's taken my excuse, but bad because I worry what he's up to. I didn't have to cancel tonight on the girls in the end because Kelly is finally telling Josh about the baby, Eve is on a date with Greg, and Kara is visiting her mum in Manchester for the weekend, so as I get into the bath, I feel relieved that I can just stay home.

I decide to order some food shopping because I have no food here, so I use my phone to arrange a delivery for tomorrow. That way I don't have to go out either.

I can't stop thinking about my face. It looks better, but you can still see the rough outline of a handprint, and around my eye, there are patches of bright red and yellow. I close my eyes and turn the hot water on with my foot. I keep thinking about seeing mum and dad tomorrow and if I can cover my face enough so they don't notice. But then, to be honest, I don't know if I even want to go out. I feel anxious about leaving my house. No one can get me here...

What's happening to me?

I start falling asleep in the bath so I get out. I throw on my pink lounge-wear and after turning on the TV in my bedroom, get into bed and snuggle under the duvet. I curl up on my side and mindlessly flick through the TV channels, settling on the Tattoo Fixers. I love this programme.

My phone vibrates on the bedside table so I reach over and grab it.
Neymar.
 - Where are you? -
I groan inwardly. *Not now.*
I type a quick reply.
 - Home. Tired. -
I focus back on the TV and my phone buzzes again.
 - Can I come over? -
 - No. -
 - Why? -
 - Cuz I'm tired. Come over tomorrow. -
 - Now?
For God sake, why can't he take no for an answer?
 - Really? I've just got comfortable. Come tomorrow. -
 - 5 mins? -
I growl as I read his text. That means I have to put on makeup and everything, For God's sake!
 - Fine. When r u coming? -

CHAPTER 10

I RELUCTANTLY ROLL out of bed to grab my makeup bag. My phone vibrates, but I start applying foundation to my face before I check it. I've actually got quite good at this.

I hear knocking at the door and panic. He was outside this whole time, are you serious?

I spread the foundation over my face and quickly rub it in. The knocking starts again.

"Two minutes," I shout and then quickly apply some eyeshadow. The knocking starts to wind me up, so after quickly applying some mascara, I go and answer the door.

I crack it open and see Neymar standing there in all black, looking sexy as hell, holding a paper bag with *Lolas* on it. I try not to roll my eyes as I let him in and close the door behind him. I don't turn the light on and I'm hoping he gets the hint and leaves.

"Layla."

I turn to face him and pretend to yawn. "Neymar."

"I know you've been feeling tired, so I thought I'd bring you some soup." He lifts the paper bag and hits me with a beautifully sincere smile. I'm angry with him, but I can't help but smile back. *He's being sweet.*

He offers me the bag and I take it. "Thank you."

I take it into the kitchen and put it on the side. He follows behind me and turns the light on. I panic and turn to face him, squinting as the light stings my eyes. "Turn it off!"

"What the fuck, Layla?" And he's right in front of me. I turn away to step around him, but I only make it to the doorway before he grabs my arm and pulls me around to face him. "What are you hiding?" he asks, his deep voice sounding unusually cold.

"Nothing." I need a story and quickly. Damn it, I can't *think* around him. This is why I didn't want to see him.

"Don't lie to me." I take a quick look at him before I cross my arms. He smells so good... My stomach knots. He's clearly angry but the concern on his face tugs at my feelings.

I sigh heavily. "It's nothing, okay? Just leave it."

"Layla..."

"Please, Neymar." I rub my face in my hands but stupidly forget about my eye and hiss, quickly pulling them away. It hurts.

"What the fuck happened, Layla?"

"Stop saying my name like that, Neymar!" His tone frustrates me; I can't take it. There is always some unspoken words when he says my fucking name.

"So help me fucking God, if you don't tell me how the fuck you hurt your face."

"I didn't hurt it!" I snap. "Since I met you all I've done is get my face fucked up! Fuck!" I wince in pain as I turn away from him. This wasn't meant to happen! He wasn't meant to see me like this. I lean against the door frame and close my eyes. I need to calm down.

"Please..." he tries again, softly, standing close behind me. "Tell me what happened. Is this why you cancelled on me?"

I nod, suddenly feeling overwhelmed. He walks past me into the kitchen and runs the tap for a while before returning and standing in front of me. Tears pool in my eyes and when he lifts my chin, they fall down my cheeks. His expression is so intense that I focus my eyes on the door frame. I can't bear to see the look on his face.

He lifts a wet tea towel to my face and starts wiping away my makeup. He's gentle; his touch surprisingly light. He inhales sharply after a while of wiping and I swallow hard, crying silently as he wipes my cheek and then around my eye.

"When did this happen?" he asks quietly and wipes away more of my tears.

I sigh heavily and admit defeat. "Thursday night."

"Thursday?" He looks horrified. "And it still looks like *this?*" I can tell he's trying to control his temper but is clearly struggling. "Tell me what happened."

"Please, just leave it."

"Tell me."

"It does–"

"Layla," he warns.

I take a deep breath and he releases my face. "I was walking to the taxi rank after meeting Kelly. Some boys walked past and one of them recognised me from being..." I bite my lip and hesitate, unsure if I should really tell him this...

"Go on."

"Neymar, I–"

"Go. On."

I sigh. "One of them recognised me from being in the car park from that night. He said I better not tell anyone about what happened and then he slapped me. Said it was a warn–"

"He's a fucking dead man," he shouts, stepping around me. I jump at his sudden outburst and then turn and watch as he walks towards my front door and clenches a fist to punch my wall.

I gasp in shock; he's raging. I stare in silence at the back of him as he struggles to control himself. I start looking around at my things, ready to protect anything he might smash up.

"You're coming with me," he says icily.

"What?"

He turns and glares at me. "Put some shoes on. You are coming with me."

What? I'm not even dressed, and I don't want to go with him. "Ne–"

"Shoes," he demands, and his tone makes me shudder. He's practically seething.

I find some Ugg's in my under-stairs cupboard and put on a coat with a hood. I walk over to the side table and pick up my keys and then follow him out to the car. Neymar opens the door and I get inside, giving Jay a perfect view of my face.

"Hey– What the fuck, Layla?" he says and follows me with his eyes until I'm out of view behind him. He then stares at Neymar while he gets in and shuts the door. "Bruv?"

"Them little fuckin' pussies from the car park seen Layla up town." He pulls out his phone and starts furiously tapping on it.

"Shit, Layla, you okay?" Jay asks while looking in his rear-view. His eyes meet mine and I nod before looking out the window. Why do I feel so guilty when it's not even my fault? I was just there by coincidence that night and now look at me.

I hear Neymar on the phone. "Yeah, I wanna know where Deano is and his group of little pussy friends. Find him." He hangs up. I turn to face him and he looks up from his phone to look at me, too. His eyes leave mine and I can see that he's looking at my face. My heart sinks as his jawline tenses and he looks away from me.

He can't even look at me.

We sit in the car in silence. It's so uncomfortable. I keep my gaze fixed outside. Neymar's phone rings and he answers it. I hear the sound of someone talking but can't make out what is said.

"I will... meet me there, and bring them tings," he says before hanging up. "Elephant and Castle," he tells Jay.

The car is deathly quiet as we drive through Central to South. Neymar texts on his phone but doesn't say a word. I feel so bad and regret opening my mouth.

Why didn't I just ignore his text?

Neymar gives Jay a street name and then soon after, we're pulling up across the street from a chicken shop. I see the group of boys inside. I panic and pray to God that he doesn't make me get out. Other cars pull up in front of us and dread fills me.

"Which one was it?" I hear Neymar ask, his voice void of emotion. I feel Jay looking in the rear-view mirror at me, but I avoid eye contact.

"Please, Neymar, let's jus–"

"Which one was it, Layla?"

"Neymar, please, I–"

"Which one was it?" I jump at his voice. I look over him to the shop and point him out.

"The one in the red hat." A sob slips from my lips. I feel like I've just signed that boy's death warrant.

"Jay, take Layla home."

"Neymar, please, don't do this," I beg him. I grab his arm and he turns to look at me. He focuses on my face and then pulls his arm away before getting out. He walks to the car in front and Jay indicates to pull off. Men get out from the other cars and I see Neymar chatting to them as we drive into the road.

I turn to look out of the back window and watch them run across the street and into the takeaway.

This is all my fault...

I cry silently all the way home. Jay looks through his rear view at me nuff times but I can't face him. I feel awful. My life has been such a mess since I met Neymar, but he also makes me feel so alive inside. I should leave him alone, but I just can't.

I get out the car when we get to mine and slam the door behind me. I run up the steps, get into my house and run straight upstairs. After crawling into bed, I cry into my blanket and think about that boy. I wonder if he'll be okay.

What have I done?

A part of me feels like he deserves it for what he did to me, but when I think about how angry Neymar was...

As I start to fall asleep, the only thing I can think about is the fact I snitched on that boy.

You're a snitch, Layla. Something you always said you'd never be.

CHAPTER 11

MY PHONE RINGS on the pillow beside me, waking me up. It's Neymar. I let it ring out but it rings again. I look at the clock, it's two in the morning. I groan. I can't deal with this right now... I hear knocking on the door and ignore it but he keeps calling my phone so after the eighth time, I answer.

"What?"

"Let me in."

"I'm sleeping."

"Let me in, Layla."

I kiss my teeth before I hang up. *He's driving me mental.*

I go downstairs and stand at the door. I'm worried about the state he might be in. I crack it open and see him staring at the ground; he's wearing different clothes but still all in black.

He looks up at me and my stomach tightens. As much as I need to stay away from him, it's impossible, even just for the way he makes me feel. I open the door wider and he walks in without a word. I close it and hesitate before I eventually turn around to face him.

I feel so nervous as his eyes wander over my body before returning to my face. His fists clench and I know, he's still mad.

"Do you want a drink?" I ask, feeling the need to break the tense silence.

"No."

I nod slowly, then cross my arms. Are we just going to have a stand-off then?

"Why didn't you tell me?" He sounds hurt.

"Because, I knew you'd be angry."

"Too fucking right, I'm angry. He put his hands on you..." He looks up at the ceiling and I can feel the rage radiating off him.

"Calm down, please."

His head snaps forward. "Calm down? He fucking did that to you!"

"And I'm sure you did him worse," I mutter, accusing him of the worst.

"He got what he asked for."

I sigh in torment. "And now I'm going to have to live with the fact that I snitched on him and got him fucked up because of it."

"He deserved everything he got, Jesus, you feel bad for him?" The look on his face is of pure horror. Shocked doesn't cover it.

I don't say anything and it seems to annoy him.

"You *do?*"

I walk past him to go to the kitchen. I see the soup on the table so warm it in the microwave. He stands at the kitchen door and watches me while I take out a spoon and fill a glass with water.

"Most girls–"

"I'm not most girls and if you're assuming that I am, then you should leave," I say simply, just as the timer on the microwave goes off. I open the door and the smell of the soup fills the room. I'm hungry and it smells so good.

"I know you aren't, and I didn't mean it like–"

"So what *do* you mean?" I ask, cutting him off again. I pull out a chair and sit down at the table with the soup. I hear him sigh and it pulls at my conscience. "Do you want some?"

"No. I got it for you."

"Don't lie, I know you want some." I look up at him. His gaze is intense and we have a silent passing of words before he sits down at the table with me.

I stir the soup before scooping up a piece of fish and some broth to blow it. When I feel it's cooled enough, I slip it into my mouth. It's so nice, and easy on my jaw as well.

"That is not even hot," he scolds me.

"It is."

I know he's rolled his eyes but I ignore him. I take another mouthful and then slide the plastic container across the table to him. He eats a few spoonful's without blowing it and I cringe. "You are not normal."

"It's not hot."

I shake my head. "Why did you come here earlier?"

"You cancelled our appointment, I was worried. I bought you the soup to make you feel better."

He takes a spoonful of the soup and blows on it before offering it to me. I eat it and he repeats.

"It is making me feel better, thank you," I say softly.

"Layla, I'm sorry for all this. This is exactly the reason why I don't want you getting mixed up in my shit."

"What are we doing, Neymar?" He offers me more soup and I take it.

He looks at me and frowns.

I swallow my mouthful of soup and then take a deep breath. "We're clearly bad for each other. You have too much baggage, and I keep getting my face messed up. I'm starting to feel like someone else, all I do is lie and cry, or get hurt."

He rests the spoon in the soup and rubs his face in his hands. I take him in. His short hair perfectly faded behind his ear and the soft skin on his neck... *my* ink on his neck... the angel disappearing under his t-shirt.

I exhale and it sounds as tormented as I feel. I can't stay away from him, even if I wanted to. I find everything about him so forbidden and the more I try to tell myself I don't want to be with him, the more I feel like I need him.

He pulls his hands from his face and looks me.

"I wanted to leave you alone, but I missed you. I wanted to call you late yesterday night but I didn't, and then today, I came here... and your face. I'm vexed you never told me. I thought you were avoiding me."

"Well, I kinda was. I knew you'd lose your shit if you saw my face. The boys at the studio have been doing my head in about it and I didn't need you flying off the handle."

"I don't want you keeping secrets from me, Layla."

"You keep secrets from me," I throw back in return.

"I don't hide things from you, I just don't tell you things, there's a difference."

I bite my lip nervously. "I want to stay away from you. I know you're going to hurt me, but every time I see you... I can't explain how you make me feel." And that kiss... God, I can't stop thinking about that kiss. My eyes flicker to his lips and I suppress a moan. I remember I was so wet afterwards.

"I know what you're thinking." I watch his soft lips part before returning my eyes to his. He shrugs off his jacket so it falls onto the back of the chair. He pushes his chair out and then grabs my hand off the table.

"Come here," he orders.

I step over to him and he pulls me to straddle him. He looks up at me with wanting eyes and settles his hands on my naked waist.

"We should stay away from each other," he says thoughtfully while caressing my waist.

"Yes."

He pulls down on my hips and I feel his hardness through his jeans. My breathing quickens instantly and so does his. His eyes are like an abyss... so much depth... endless...

"I can't," he says before pulling me towards him and kissing my lips.

I close my eyes and let him ravish my wanting mouth. His hands are all over my skin and I sigh with relief. I hold the back of his neck and his hands roam up my top to my naked breasts. The feeling inside me intensifies and I moan into his mouth when his tongue caresses mine. He groans and clutches my top in his hands and pulls it up over my head.

His lips are back on mine and his hands are on my aching skin. He handles me expertly and I gasp when he pinches my straining nipples. I pull my lips from his and pull his t-shirt up. He leans forward so I can get it over his head and then he pulls me against him so our bodies are skin to skin. *Oh god...* His mouth finds my neck and I look up at my ceiling to give him better access. He plants soft kisses on my skin, down my neck, my chest and to the tops of my breasts. He kneads them with his palms and then directs one into his hot, wet mouth.

"*Oh fuck,*" I moan and close my eyes.

Little groans rumble from inside him as he sucks and nips at my delicate flesh. One of his hands finds my waist and he pulls me down so that the bulge in his jeans rubs against me. I moan as the friction makes my hips jerk uncontrollably.

"Layla?"

"Mmhh?" I look down and he suddenly pulls away.

"Are you sure about this?" I see the hesitation on his face and I know that he is really asking himself that question and not me.

I rest my forehead against his and sigh deeply. "We don't have to." I get up off his lap and turn my back to him. I quickly pull on my cropped top and then turn and hand him his shirt. "You should go."

"Layla, I'm sorry."

"You seem to be sorry a lot."

He looks hurt as he takes his t-shirt from me.

"I'm going to bed. You can see yourself out." I leave the soup on the table and him in the kitchen. When I settle into bed I hear the door quietly close as he leaves. I feel angry more than anything. Why won't he have sex with me? Is he seeing someone else? It doesn't make sense. I groan and close my eyes. That was so hot, though, *ugh.* Why did he have to open his mouth and speak?

I close my eyes and try to sleep but I keep feeling his hands all over me. I feel so frustrated with everything. My life used to be so simple. Work during the week, get drunk and fuck on the weekends... now... I feel like all I do is lust over a man that has a steel-like sense of control.

CHAPTER 12: NEYMAR

I CLOSE THE DOOR quietly behind me. My wood is so fucking hard; I'm even walking fucked up.

Layla is fuckin' sexy, and them noises she was making had me all up in my shit... I should've just fucked her, Jesus. Why the fuck didn't I? I know she wanted it, too. The disappointment on her face after I asked that question said enough for the both of us.

I get into the car and tell Jay to take me home.

"Is she okay?"

"Yeah. Seams to be." Fuck this woman, she brings out the worst in me but also the best. "She's driving me crazy, I swear, Jay." My wood is still raging. It's getting almost impossible to say no to her now. The more I see her the more I want to fuck her.

"She's nice, that's probably why you like her. She ain't like the skets we usually smash. She didn't even wanna point out Deano."

"I know." That's true. I wish I never met her. No... I don't mean that, but I'm dying here. It's her eyes, those innocent brown eyes, they look straight fucking through me, through all the fake and bullshit. She don't know what I'm like, but she's still got time for me. She wants to know *me*.

I think about the night I met her and the way she looked at me. She was so vulnerable. When she cried, I didn't know what the fuck to do, but I know it hurt me. Girls cry around me all the time, but I've never felt like that.

"I guess we know why she hasn't been leaving the house."

"Yeah." The thought of her face makes me angry as fuck.

"What you gonna do, you gonna stay away from her?"

"Don't say dumb shit, Jay."

He laughs but I don't. "I need her to finish this ink first."

"You're playing with fire, man."

"You don't think I know that? I just need to stay focused and get out of this shit."

"What we did tonight is not gonna help that."

"I know, but what was I meant to do? You saw her fucking face! That bitch deserved what he got." *I would have done worse if I had the time.*

"Did you tell her?"

"Don't be stupid." I'm sure she knows, though. *That woman just knows shit.*

"You need to be careful."

"Once we go legit and the deal with the East goes through, we'll be chilling."

"The money is almost clean, then you can sign the deeds."

"It's not happening quick enough." I can't fuck Layla until I'm out of this shit. I don't want to hurt her and since she told me about her brother, I'm more determined than ever to leave this life behind. I'm twenty-seven. I need to grow up. I've lived my life in these streets since I was ten, I don't wanna do it no more.

"I think she's good for you. She's independent as well, not like these money hoes. You know you're making it when you can get a woman who makes you better, instead of dragging you down all the time."

"She isn't my woman." Saying that vexes me, but it's true.

"Right. But you won't let her be anyone else's either."

I glare at him.

"Just admit it, man. You've had me following her and all sorts."

Yeah, but at first it was just to make sure she kept her mouth shut and didn't talk to nobody. Now, I actually care about the woman. "Well, you ain't been following her that well have you cuz that little pussy Deano managed to get to her."

"I explained that, Bruv, I wasn't even working Thursday night." He gets defensive.

"I don't give a fuck. I want eyes on her at all times and you make sure Kimani knows that, too."

"I'll talk to him."

"Make fucking sure."

"I will."

CHAPTER 13

I WAKE UP and look at the clock. It's just after one, but I feel like I've hardly slept at all. Thank God it's a bank holiday tomorrow.

I text my mum and dad to tell them I'm busy with work so I won't be visiting this weekend. I promise to see them next weekend and they seem happy enough.

I reply to some work emails and then text Kelly. She was meant to tell Josh about the baby last night but I haven't heard from her.

- Hey babe, everything okay? Xx -

She replies quickly.

- U were right, he's buzzing! Xx -

- I told you. So happy for you both. Xx -

I can't help but feel a twinge of envy when I think of how lucky she is to have Josh. I text Eve and Kara and then Kara calls me.

"Hey," I answer.

"Hey, babe, you okay?"

"Yeah, I'm good. How's Manchester?"

"Good, it's nice to see the folks."

"Yeah, I bet."

"I wanted to ask if you could send me some money. My wages haven't gone in and I'm broke. I'll send it you back on Monday."

"Yeah, that's fine, babe. Everything okay at work?"

"Yeah fine. My boss is just an alcoholic prick who can't pay us on time, but apart from that…"

I laugh and she cusses me out. "Sorry. I'll do it now, okay? How much do you need?"

"Three hundred? I wanna do some shopping."

"That's fine."

"I'll get you something."

"Will look forward to it."

"Okay, babe. Text you later."

"Okay, Hun. Later."

I log into my mobile banking and transfer the money. It says to allow up to two hours but it always goes in straight away. I send her a quick text to say I've done it and then go for a shower. After getting dressed in a pair of leggings and a vest, I get back into bed and watch a few films. I feel bored being at home, but I also still feel nervous about going out. I know I need to break the cycle and leave the house before it becomes a problem, but I'm too scared.

I decide to be productive and sketch out some designs for the work emails I've received. I spend the early evening scanning in the designs and sending them to potential customers. I get a text from Maverick telling me they made over a grand extra yesterday and I smile as I read it. I've come so far, but I couldn't have done it without them. They've been so supportive since I opened my studio and hired them. I knew they'd be the perfect fit for my studio.

When I finish sending the emails from my laptop I hear knocking at my door. I panic but remember I ordered shopping yesterday. I check my face in the mirror, *I forgot about my face.* God knows what this delivery guy is gonna think.

I open the door and he looks at my face in shock. He stammers to say hello and then hands me the paperwork to sign. "Just two substitutions, love."

I nod and read the top of the paper. No loose Bananas so a pack of five have been provided and no Cadburys Dairy Milk so they've given me Galaxy. I rummage through the bags and hand him back the chocolate. I only eat *Cadbury's.*

"Can you sign here please?" he asks, handing me his Epad.

I use the plastic pen to sign in the box and hand it back to him. "Thank you," I say grabbing all my bags from the crates and closing the door.

I put away my shopping and throw the leftover soup in the bin from last night. I stare at the chair in the kitchen. Last night was so hot. I wish he had of just given it to me. His hands felt so good on my body. I can tell that he knows how to fuck a girl good and I know I want that in my life—even though I shouldn't.

I sigh deeply and hear my phone ringing upstairs. After running up the stairs two at a time, it stops ringing as I reach the landing. Once in my bedroom, I sit on my bed and scroll down my screen to see two missed calls from Neymar. He calls again as I look at my phone but I just stare at it for a moment, thinking about how much of a pussy tease he is.

Ugh... "Hello?" I answer. *I just don't learn.*

"Hey, you good?"

"I'm fine. You?"

"Yeah, good."

"Good."

Silence stretches between us. I wonder what he's calling for.

"What you doing?" he asks after a while.

"Nothing. I just put my shopping delivery away, and I guess I'm gonna make some dinner."

"You wanna meet me over West? I wanna show you something."

"West London?"

"Yeah."

Panic fills me. I know deep down that I don't have to worry about bumping into that boy again but meeting him still means taking a taxi, and then walking somewhere... on my own... "I can't," I blurt out.

"Layla, what's wrong?"

"I'm sorry. I just wanna stay home." *Forever...*

"When did you last go out?"

"Yesterday, with you."

"That don't count."

"I've been to work," I insist.

"Is this because of your face?" he asks quietly.

"Umm, yeah. Kinda."

"Tell me why you don't wanna come out."

I sigh. He wants me to be honest so I decide to tell him the truth. "The thought of going out on my own scares me."

I hear his sharp intake of breath. "I'll come get you. When can you be ready?"

"Um, a half-hour?"

"See you then," he says before hanging up.

I have a quick shower to freshen up and then do my makeup the best I can. I check my face in the mirror before I get dressed and unless you knew me, you wouldn't be able to tell that my face is mash-up. I smile at my work. I've done my smoky eyes, curled the ends of my hair and opted for a simple little black dress and heels because I don't know where we're going, and I don't want to look like a slut next to him.

I pack a clutch bag and then make my way downstairs to see Neymar's silhouette through my smoked glass door. I open it and see him dressed in a black shirt and jeans. Those buttons are open again and I can't help but check him out... He looks fine as hell and I sigh deeply.

He smirks and I scorn him for getting kicks out of my frustration.

"You look amazing," he says with a twinkle in his eye. The use of the word amazing is not lost on me and my frown quickly turns into a smile.

"Thank you."

He offers me his hand and after picking up my keys off the side I take it and let him walk me down the steps. I look for the range but it's not here. He leads me across the street to a black Audi instead.

I've never really been a fan of Audi's. He opens the passenger door for me to get in and I slip inside. He closes my door and a few seconds later he's in the car beside me pressing the ignition. Rick Ross plays on the stereo but he swiftly switches it to Capital FM.

It's slow jam night and just as *Pony* by *Ginuwine* finishes, *Usher, Can you handle it,* plays. I look out the window and listen to the lyrics of the song. I remember this song word-for-word from the *Confessions Album* but now I'm really hearing the lyrics, I swear this song was made for Neymar and me. I sigh deeply as we pass cars on the dual carriageway. I feel affected by this song and I wonder if he feels it, too.

"You okay?"

I turn to face him. He looks too big to drive this car. "Yeah." I'm so *not* okay, I never am any more.

"Aren't you going to compliment my car?" he asks with mock hurt while changing lanes.

"I don't really like Audi's."

I watch the surprise spread across his face. "How can you not like *this* Audi?" He sounds surprised.

I shrug. "I don't know. I just don't like them. Have I hurt your feelings now?" I ask playfully.

"Always." He glances at my body before returning his attention back to the road.

His eyes always make me feel naked. *How does he do that?*

"So, tell me why you haven't been leaving your yard?"

I roll my eyes at his question but I'll answer him. If it's honesty he wants from me then he can have it from now on. "I don't feel safe on my own," I say and his expression changes. "So much has happened in the last few weeks. After Thursday, I only managed to go to work and back because I didn't want to let any of my customers down."

"You ain't got to worry about him no more, y'know that, right?" he says reassuringly, taking a quick look at me.

My stomach knots as he confirms my suspicions.

"Don't be worrying about that shit either. He had it coming for long and if you hadn't of shown up that night, he would've been duppied from then."

I bite my lip nervously. *That doesn't make me feel any less to blame.* I just want to know if he did it, or if one of the others did. When he came to mine last night he didn't have any marks on him and I *definitely* would have noticed...

"What are you thinking about now?"

"If you did it."

"Do you really wanna know the answer to that question?"

My stomach turns. "You just answered it, anyway." I sigh and briefly close my eyes.

Why the fuck have I gotten myself into this situation?

"You haven't eaten?" he asks changing the subject.

"No."

"We can eat when we get there."

"Where are we going?"

"To a place that will hopefully change this situation between you and me." He looks nervous as he drives but I'm intrigued.

"What situation is that then?"

"You know exactly the one."

His no sex rule... he must be talking about that...

"While we're there, try to call me Jackson, if you can."

"Okay," I reply, not questioning him further. I'm guessing he doesn't go by his real name much, or maybe Neymar isn't his real name. "Is Neymar your real name?"

"Yeah." He seems surprised by my question. "You think I gave you a fake name?"

"I don't hear anyone else calling you Neymar, so I just wondered.

He smiles and I smirk at him. "What?"

"The way your mind works."

CHAPTER 14

WE ARRIVE IN THE WEST END. It's heaving and people randomly wander out into the street in front of us. Neymar comes to a stop outside a tall, blue building in the middle of a row of clubs. I've not been inside before but I know that this is club Entourage. Butterflies swarm in my stomach at the number of people queueing to get in. I always feel nervous if I go out clubbing without drinking first, but tonight I feel even more anxious.

My door is opened and I jump.

"It's good. He's with me," Neymar says softly and rests his hand on my thigh. I relax and watch Neymar get out his side before getting out myself.

"Miss," a man says dressed in a suit.

"Thanks." I walk around the car and meet Neymar on the pavement. He holds my hand firmly and takes us up to the club entrance.

"Jackson," two men greet him as they lift the rope and let us through.

He hands one of them his car key. "Sort that out, please, boss."

"No problem."

Neymar squeezes my hand reassuringly as he leads me up a sky-blue set of stairs. My heart is racing from nerves. *I need a really strong drink.*

"You alright?" he asks tentatively as we reach the top.

"Yep," I answer, trying to sound nonchalant. I wonder if he can tell that I'm not.

We're greeted by two men at the next set of double doors who refer to him by his known name. They open the doors to a sea of people dancing in front of us and a long glass bar on the right-hand side. I look up and there are glass windows either side of a high ceiling and what I can see, three more floors. My legs feel heavy as I watch all the people. I feel so scared.

He tugs on my hand and I look up at him. "Hungry?"

I nod and he pulls me rightwards towards a man standing in front of an elevator. When he sees us approaching, he presses a button and the doors open for us to step inside, without breaking stride.

Once inside, Neymar presses four on the number pad and I sigh with relief when the door closes.

"I ain't gonna let anything happen to you again, Layla."

I look at him but he's already staring at me. I believe him. "I know."

"We can go back to yours if you want?"

"No, I'll be fine once I get a drink in me."

He smiles but it's a sad one. "I can help you with that."

I involuntarily squeeze his hand when we reach the top floor and the doors open. I relax when I see the room is much less busy than the one below. The smell of the food hits me and as we step out, I see tables against a wall of floor-to-ceiling windows, giving an amazing view of West London.

"It's beautiful." The words come out all by themselves.

"Second best view in the house," Neymar replies before we are led to a table right by the window. There are only four other occupied tables in here so even though music is playing, it feels really intimate.

"What can I get you to drink?" the waitress asks as we sit down.

"Ciroc, please, Amaretto," I tell her. Neymar smiles and tells her to bring a bottle. I rest my chin on my knuckles and look out into the city. The lights twinkle far away in the distance, and you can even see the London eye from here. I know Eve has been here with work and I've heard this place is a hot-spot for the rich and famous. It's strange because I've been to the club next door and the two buildings are completely different.

"So, you like it?" Neymar asks after a while.

"I love this view." I could get so much inspiration for my work looking out there with my sketch pad.

"I want to buy it."

"This club?" I whisper across the table to him.

"Here's your, Ciroc. Are you ready to order?"

"Not yet," Neymar answers for us.

"No problem." She walks away and I look back at Neymar.

"The current owner's selling, so I'm working some things out to take it over."

Shit... so this is what he meant. He's gonna give up the streets and go legit. This place must be worth a lot. Selfishly, I hope he does sell it because hopefully then he'll feel like we can move on from just messing with each other. He must have been running everything for a long time to be even close to being able to afford this place though, which also means he's been involved in a lot of shit.

"It's a lot."

He laughs and pours us both a drink. "It's a lot. I know."

"Well, if this is what you want, then good for you." I nervously play with a strand of loose hair.

His eyes narrow. "That's it?"

"What do you mean?" I frown, not understanding.

"You're not gonna ask questions?"

"No. It's none of my business and I have one of my own to mind." He must be so nervous about this and I don't want to make him feel any more of anything else. I remember how I felt parting with the money for the studio, and that was nowhere near as much money as this place must be worth. "You have to put me and my girls on the guest list for this place, though, when it's yours."

He laughs and I look at his mouth. *Ugh...* "So that's all you're thinkin' about? Getting on the guest list?"

And under you. "Yeah, my girls usually get me on guest lists, this is my one chance to outdo them all in one go." I smile sweetly at him then chuckle, making him roll his eyes.

"I will put you *all* permanently on the guest list, if I get it, alright?"

I wonder if that means I'll finally be able to get into his private VIP as well. "Deal," I say and offer my hand.

He looks surprised. "What *exactly* are we shaking on?"

"To me getting what I want."

His eyes look down from my face momentarily before shaking my hand. "Deal."

Neymar orders our food. We don't get any starters but we both have risotto for main and then I ask for sorbet for dessert.

"Don't you like sweet things?" I ask him as I enjoy the icy cold sorbet.

His eyes burn me. "Yeah, just not anything on this menu."

"So what would you choose for a dessert, if you could have anything in the world?" I slip a mouthful of sorbet into my mouth and let it melt on my tongue before swallowing the liquid. He studies me intently while he thinks about his choice.

"New York cheesecake."

"Really?" I ask feeling slightly disappointed. "Out of anything, you would choose that?" I eat more of my sorbet. Turning the spoon over in my mouth and pulling it out upside down. It tastes good, there's a good lemon kick to it. I watch him looking at me so I offer him some.

He shakes his head. "Wanna shot this Ciroc with me?"

"What about the car?"

"Jay will pick us up." He shares out some of the Ciroc between our glasses and on his count of three, we drink. The amaretto taste is strong and I can almost feel the alcohol shooting up my veins when it reaches my belly.

"I'm not nervous any more," I confess quietly, feeling my belly warm.

"Good, wanna finish the tour?"

I nod and he smiles.

We leave the restaurant and stop on the third floor—the exclusive floor. People have to pay five grand just to get in here. It's quiet because it's still early so we make our way down to the next floor, the VIP.

Neymar leads me out of the elevator into a room playing my favourite music. Afro Beats. It's not *too* busy here and even though I want to stop several times to dance, we easily make it through the dance floor and up to the bar without any problems.

He leans into my ear and slips his hand around my lower back.

Damn, he smells good.

"You wanna stay on Ciroc with me?"

I whisper back a yes in his ear before he moves away, making sure to brush his neck with my lips. I know he's affected by the way he looks at me when he straightens up.

He asks for a bottle of Ciroc to go to a table before taking my hand again. The music and the alcohol are making me feel good, so when we reach the dance floor, I pull his hand so he stops. I bite my lip nervously and start to move gently with the music. He watches me but doesn't say no.

I move closer to him and smile shyly. The drink has made me brave with him, plus, the music always makes me wanna dance when I go out. He reaches out his hand and I press it to my waist. When I wrap my arms around his neck, his other hand finds my ass. I move my hips to the rhythm of *Korede Bello, Do like that.* He moves in time with me and then spins me around so that my back is pressed to his chest. I lean my head back and grind my ass against his body. His hands are on me and every memory I have of him touching me rushes through my mind. He moves his hips and I am soon aroused by the way he grinds and how well he holds my body...

Fuck this, I can't do it.

I stop dancing and pull his hand to continue towards the booths. He looks surprised but follows me. We arrive at a small table and after I slip in, he follows. The booth is next to the glass wall and if I look down, I can see the open part of the club below.

"Do you spend a lot of time here?" I ask completely uninterested while trying to get the intense urge to fuck him out of my mind.

"No."

"So how did you know about, y'know?"

He sighs and then looks troubled. "I've been looking for something for a while. I know a lot of people and one of them told me about this place."

"Ah, okay," I reply. He pours our drinks and I take a sip. Maybe another bottle of this wasn't such a good idea. I've been feeling the effects of the Ciroc for a while now but I'm trying to hide it. I'm grateful my alcohol threshold is quite high, and I guess eating upstairs helped.

"Why do you do what you do?" he asks, sitting closer to me. He's definitely all up in my personal space but I'm not as nervous around him now, not compared to the first time we were at a club together.

"I've just always loved drawing. As far back as I can remember, I would sketch. When I was at school and I experimented with that Indian ink. I guess my love for tattoos was born. Art school just seemed like the right thing to do and then I practised until a guy called Nick gave me a job in his studio. The rest..." I shrug.

"And look at you now."

"Yeah, I've done well."

He smiles and my eyes fix on his lips. I really want to kiss him. He runs his fingers through my hair at the side of my face and my heart races. The alcohol is making me want him more. He leans down to kiss me and I am left utterly breathless when he pulls away.

"You turn me on, *fuck*," he says hoarsely.

"You do, too." I close my eyes and take a deep breath. I feel so fucking horny right now. I press my legs together; I'm wet...

"I'm trying," he says and when I look up at him, I get lost in those eyes.

"I know."

AN HOUR OR SO LATER, we leave the club where Jay is kerbside waiting for us. Neymar opens my door and I get into the familiar range, with him following close behind.

"Layla," Jay greets me.

"Hey, Jay. Please excuse me, I'm a little pissed."

"As long as you had a good time, right?"

A smile quickly spreads across my lips. "I did." I look beside me at Neymar. He's already looking at me. "What?"

"Nothing," he says defensively before turning to Jay. "Jay, you know where to go."

His fingers interlock with mine and I feel emotionally buzzing. Considering where we were at the start of the night, I feel like we've made good progress, sort of. I lay my head back on the seat and close my eyes but start to feel sad the longer the journey goes on because I'm gonna have to say goodbye to Neymar.

He squeezes my hand and I open my eyes to look out of the window. We're on my road already. I sigh as Jay pulls up and then thank him for the lift. Like usual, Neymar gets out first and I follow. He wraps his arm around my waist and then we walk up the steps together to my door.

"Thanks for tonight," I tell him as I slip my key into the lock and open my door. I look up at him and he's looking at me, too. I bite my lip and try to hide my feelings. I don't want him to know how sad I feel to see him go.

"Do you want me to stay with you tonight?" he asks cautiously while brushing a few strands of stray hair away from the side of my face.

Oh shit!

I nod straight away. "I won't try anything."

He smirks and motions for Jay to go and then we go inside.

"Are you hungry?" I ask him, feeling nervous.

"No, I'm alright."

He hovers in the doorway to the kitchen while I run myself a glass of water and pop two paracetamol. Afterwards, we go upstairs to my bedroom and as promised, I don't try it on with him. I'm just grateful he's here. I get changed into shorts and a vest in my bathroom and when I come back into my room, he's already in my bed with no shirt on.

Oh, God… look at that body…

Seriously, I need to get myself together.

Deep breath…

"Make yourself comfortable why not," I say sarcastically.

"I will." His eyes slowly work their way down my body and I blush at how he makes me feel. I quickly climb into bed beside him and sit up against the headboard, mimicking him.

"You wanna fall asleep to a film?" I suggest.

"You got Netflix?"

"Yeah." I smile.

"What you smiling about?"

"Netflix and *no* chill, yeah?"

He laughs and the sound makes me happy. I grab the remote and scroll through the films. "What kinda film you wanna watch?" I ask.

"You can choose."

"Thanks." I roll my eyes and feel his hand slide onto my thigh. I try and concentrate on finding a film but it's like my brain has malfunctioned and I end up mindlessly pressing the down button on the remote without even paying attention to the screen.

"Go back," he says softly, pulling me from my daydream.

I flick up two films and select The Equalizer. "I love this film."

"You've seen it?"

"Yeah."

"Then choose something you haven't."

"No, it's good, I could watch this film over and over again."

"You sure?"

"Yep." I put the remote on my bedside table and then lean on Neymar's side. He wraps his arm around me and I rest my arm on his lap but quickly jerk it away when I feel his erection.

Damn.

"Ignore him. Put your arm back," he says, taking my hand and placing it on the lowest part of his stomach. His body is so fucking defined. I swallow hard. I can't help but think about what it would be like to have free access to every single part of him.

His hand gently strokes my side and I try my hardest not to think about sex.

"What are you thinking about?"

"You."

"What about me?"

"Just that this is nice."

"Just nice, yeah? Not amazing?"

"It's not amazing, *yet.*"

He laughs and I shift to look up at him. His deep brown eyes are soft and I can tell he's feeling the alcohol, too. My eyes stray to his lips and I can't help but lick mine...

"What do you want, Layla?"

I close my eyes briefly as his words caress my insides.

*What **don't** I want from you...*

His hand pulls on my waist to draw me closer to him. My stomach is still fluttering from his question.

"I want to get under you—but, I'll settle for just a kiss," I whisper.

"Layla." I can't describe the way he looks at me after that. He leans towards me and my breath catches in anticipation. I study his face as the space disappears between us and then his soft lips are on mine. We both let out a sigh as our mouths meet and I waste no time in taking the opportunity to slide my hand up his hard body. I hold him around the back of his neck while his hand on my waist slips lower to my bare thigh.

I close my eyes and let him lead. He demands my mouth and I let him. Our hunger for each other grows and after mere seconds we both have to pull away from each other. I breathe hard. He makes me crazy with want, and I know I get to him, too. His expression mirrors my own feelings but before I lose control and kiss him again, I turn back around to face the TV and rest my head on his chest.

I can feel that I'm wet. He only has to touch me and I'm soaked. *Fuck.* A frustrated sigh escapes me. "You drive me fucking crazy," I murmur.

"I could say the same about you."

I smile. I'll take that as a compliment.

CHAPTER 15

I WAKE, tangled in the hard body of Neymar. My back is to his front and his arm is draped over my hip, holding me against him. He smells so good and as I shift off my arm a little, I feel his morning wood. I can hear him sleeping softly behind me and I'm grateful he doesn't snore.

That would do my head in.

I close my eyes and enjoy the moment. I know once he wakes, he'll be leaving. It's just after ten and my body feels rested. That's the best sleep I've had in weeks. I guess that's what happens when you sleep with your problems. You know where they are so they can't worry you.

I doze for a while until I feel Neymar's hand stir against my stomach.

"Morning," he says huskily.

"Morning," I reply. His deep and husky voice makes me shiver. "Do you have to go? It's fine if you do." I tell him, trying to get in first, before him.

His arm tightens around me. "No." He digs his hardness into my back and kisses my shoulder. "You trying to get rid of me, like usual?"

"Like usual?"

"Yeah, you always tryin' to get rid of me."

"I..."

"At the club, at your studio, here."

Oh shit. So that's what he's meant by his little comments. "Well, that was then. I'm not trying to get rid of you this time." *Far from.*

"Good." His hand takes advantage of my body and he feels me in all the places he can reach.

"Neymar," I sigh desperately. "As much as I love your hands on me, I don't think that's a good idea," I mumble as his hand finds my breasts. *God.. his touch feels so good...*

"Are you feeling frustrated again?" he whispers in my ear, brushing his lips against my skin.

"Yes, but I'm also into delayed gratification now."

He laughs and it makes me smile. "Is that so?"

"I don't seem to have a choice." I can't hide the disappointment in my voice.

"You always have a choice." He kisses my neck and I moan softly. His hand slips into my shorts and I know he's going to touch me. I don't want him to get me off like this. I want cock, for fuck sake!. *Ugh... why...*

"Right, breakfast." I'm hungry. I reluctantly pull myself away from his grip and get out of bed. I raise my hands to the ceiling and stretch out my body. His eyes fix themselves to my tattoo.

"That ink is fucking sexy," he growls and rolls over onto his back. He grabs himself under the covers and groans.

I laugh. "It's just a tattoo, babe."

He looks at me out of the corner of his eye. "It's sexy. You're fucking sexy."

I take a bow. "You're welcome."

I hear him mumble something before I disappear into the bathroom to brush my teeth and wash my face. I look at my cheek... it's still improving. I decide to cover it quickly so that Neymar doesn't have to look at it. I know it makes him angry. I retie my hair into a ponytail and then find a spare toothbrush in my bathroom cabinet.

I leave the bathroom and see him typing on his phone. "Here!" I call to him and throw the toothbrush. It lands on the bed next to him. "I'm going to make something to eat. If you want a shower the towels are in there," I tell him, pointing to my dresser.

I HEAR THE SHOWER running while I make pancakes. I don't even know if he eats pancakes, maybe I should have asked him... I decide to make eggs and toast as well, just in case, but then I worry some more in case he doesn't like eggs, so I make a fruit salad.

I hear him coming down the stairs while I'm cutting up the fruit. He comes in the kitchen but isn't wearing a shirt and although I'm happy to have the view of his body, I'm even happier because he doesn't seem in a hurry to leave.

He looks surprised at all the food.

"I didn't know what you would eat," I explain.

"Why didn't you just ask me?" He shakes his head but smiles as he sits down.

"I dunno." I frown, why didn't I just ask him?

I put the fruit on the table and sit down with him. His body is something else. "Do you go to the gym?"

"Nah, I lift at home."

"Oh, okay, so like a home gym?"

"Yeah."

I stack two pancakes on my plate, top them with fruit and then pour a little syrup on the side so I can dip my pancakes in it. "Where in London is home?"

"Not far from your studio."

"Really?" He's been close, all this time?

"Yeah. About three streets away." He puts a bit of everything on his plate and I feel good inside that I'm feeding him. He's built like a warrior, he must eat a lot.

My phone rings on the table, it's Kelly. "I need to get this," I tell him before I answer. "Hey."

"Hey, babe. You okay?"

"Yeah, I'm good." I try not to smile but I can't help it. Right now, I'm *so* okay. I blush and look at Neymar and he eyes me suspiciously. "How did it go?"

"He's so made up, babe, oh god, I can't believe I was so worried about telling him."

"I told you he'd be happy. It's so exciting!"

"I know. I still can't believe it."

My heart warms at hearing her happy. I feel Neymar's eyes on me but I keep mine down and pick my fork into my food. "When are you going to the doctors?"

"I've made an appointment for next week. Josh is coming with me."

"And so he should. When are you going to tell the girls?"

"I'm not sure yet."

"Okay, well, there's no rush and you know I won't say anything."

"I know. I'll call you later? We're going to Eileen's."

Josh's Mum's. "Of course Hun, but I'll see you Friday anyhow."

"You will."

I hang up the phone and put it on the table before looking back up at Neymar.

"Your friend?"

"Yeah, Kelly." He drifts as if in thought. "Is Jay your bestie?"

He smirks. "He's my boy, yeah."

"Is he getting out with you?" He's silent for a little while and I eat some of my fruit while I wait for him to answer.

"I hope so. We'll see."

I can tell he wants him to, but I know what these boys are like when it comes to that lifestyle. "Just focus on you."

"I am."

"Good."

We finish breakfast and he washes the dishes while I dry. This seems so normal and I can't help but smile several times. I catch him looking at me but he doesn't say anything. I wonder what goes on in that head of his. My brother would kill me if he knew that I was involved with someone like him but Neymar is trying to change and I admire that. I want to be here for him while he tries to find his way.

I WALK INTO WORK on Tuesday morning feeling happy about how the weekend went. My phone rings just before my first appointment. It's Neymar.

"Hey," I answer.

"Layla." I can tell something is off.

"What's wrong?"

"You're gonna get a visit from the pigs today."

"What? Why?" Then it hits me. That boy...

"About, y'know."

"Fuck, *Neymar*," I hiss. I go to my office and shut the door. "What do they wanna speak to me for?"

"They've seen the CCTV of him hitting you. They know we're involved so they'll try and get you to talk."

"I'm not a snitch, Neymar."

"I know. Don't watch that, alright? Tell them the truth about us, but deny everything else. If they get too heavy tell them you'll see them with a solicitor. I've got one lined up if it comes to it."

I roll my eyes. "This is the last thing I need right now. What am I gonna say about him hitting me!"

"Mistaken identity. You don't have to answer their questions, Layla."

"I know that." For God's sake.

"I gotta go but I'll see you at six. Listen, don't worry, alright. I'll sort it," he says before hanging up.

And it was going so well.

It gets to lunchtime, and while I'm sitting with Johnny eating lunch, the door goes. I turn around and see a male and female police officer standing at the door. "Can I help you?" I ask them after wiping my mouth.

"Layla Brown?" the male policeman asks.

"Yeah, that's me," I answer, feeling sick to my stomach.

"I'm Detective Jones and this is Detective Davies. Is there somewhere we can have a word?"

"Yeah, sure." I frown to act confused. I need to make them think I'm clueless. I take them into the back office and they stand while I sit at my desk.

"Do you know this man?" The woman asks while holding up a picture of the boy that hit me.

I flinch and hold my face. "Yeah. He assaulted me last week in Central and threatened to rape me."

They look at each other but I don't know what it means. "Can we ask why?"

"To be honest, I have no idea. He kept saying that he saw me somewhere and that I'd better keep my mouth shut but I have no idea what he was talking about."

"Why didn't you report it?"

"I spend a lot of time on that road, at the grill. I didn't want to cause more trouble for myself. He was clearly mistaken so I didn't think anything of it."

"Do you know a man by the name of Jackson?" Davies asks.

"I know Neymar, yeah."

"Did you tell him about being assaulted?"

Fuck. What do I say... "No, I didn't. He asked how I hurt my face, but I told him I had an accident. I haven't really known Neymar that long." I shrug.

"So, you didn't tell the man you're involved with about Deano Michaels hitting you?"

"No, I didn't. I just told you that. I don't understand, am I in trouble for not reporting it?"

"No, you're not in trouble. Did you know of Neymar before getting involved with him?"

"What is that supposed to mean?" I answer coldly. "Like I've said, I've not long known him, we only met a few weeks ago."

"If you're scared, we can help you," Jones says sympathetically.

"Scared? Why would I be scared?" I look between them, pretending to have no idea what they're talking about. I feel a lot of things about Neymar but scared is not one of them.

"Neymar Harrison is well known to us and is a very dangerous man, Layla. If I were you, I would stay as far away from him as possible."

His words piss me off and I suddenly feel very defensive. "In all due respect, officers, I'm a grown woman, thank you, and who I see in my personal time is *my* business."

They look at each other again and I cross my arms. *Fucking pigs.*

"If you do happen to remember anything else then I suggest you call us." Davies hands me a business card and I put it on my desk without looking at it.

"How *is* Dante these days?" Harris asks and I glare at him. *Okay,* so they've done their homework on me. They think they can intimidate me. Well, if they had any fucking sense they would know that I would never snitch.

"He's fine, thank you," I reply flatly, making him smile. I glare at them both. I hate the police.

"Good, we're glad to hear that. That's all for now. We'll be in touch," she says. "We can see ourselves out."

You will anyway because I wouldn't waste my time or energy escorting you. I nod and watch them leave.

I look at the clock and get even angrier because now I'm twenty minutes late for my next appointment. I can't even text Neymar because I don't want to bait him. I'll wait to speak to him when I see him later. I need to make up some fucking time now.

Johnny walks into my office just as I get up from my desk.

"What on earth was that about?"

"Nothing. Mistaken identity, I think."

"They knew your name."

"Well, it's not me they're looking for so fuck knows, Johnny. What do you want me to say?"

"The truth, Layla."

"Johnny, you know I love you, but I don't appreciate the Spanish inquisition. Just leave it, okay?"

"Okay, I'm sorry. I'm just worried about you."

"I know." I sigh. "I'm fine, okay? What they wanted has nothing to do with me."

I'VE BEEN IN A FOUL MOOD since the police questioned me and to top it off, I'm still inking when Neymar arrives at six because I wasn't able to make up the time from earlier. Neymar sits on the sofa by the door while I finish up a rose behind a girls ear. These are becoming quite popular.

When I'm done, I start cleaning down my station and I see him walking over to me while I change the needles on my iron.

"You okay?" he asks when he reaches my station.

"I'm fine." I catch Johnny looking at us while he's getting ready to leave. Neymar gets the hint and doesn't say anything else.

"I'm off now, Layla. See you in the morning," Johnny shouts over to me.

"Yes, Hun. Thanks for today."

"No problem," he replies before leaving.

As soon as the door shuts Neymar speaks. "What's wrong?" He grabs my hand as I wipe my bench. I look up at him, anger boiling inside me.

"Five-O, coming into my work and making everyone ask me twenty-million-fucking-questions, *that* is what's wrong."

"I know they came here. Why didn't you tell me?"

I kiss my teeth. "I didn't wanna bait up your phone with that shit, that's why."

"To hell with that."

I groan and snatch my hand away from him to continue wiping the surface.

"What happened?"

"They showed me a picture, asked why I never reported getting assaulted and then recommended that I stay far, far away from you." I stand up straight and cross my arms.

He smiles and it pisses me off.

"What's so funny?"

"That they said to stay away from me."

"It's not funny, and they had the cheek to ask about my brother. I know they know."

"They don't know shit, that's their problem. They thought they could come here and get you to talk."

"They said they can help me... if I'm scared." I have to hold back a snort and Neymar smirks.

"Are you scared?" I can tell that even though he's smirking, he is serious about his question.

"No."

He doesn't hide his relief at all. He walks around my bench and wraps his arm around me. "Don't worry, alright? I said I'll sort it, and I will."

I let go of my anger and hug him back. I feel safe in these arms, even if the police say he's dangerous. "Apparently you're a very dangerous man."

"I am. But they don't know I'm trying to change."

My stomach knots at his confession. I hope what Maverick said doesn't turn out to be true... "Come on, get your shirt off so I can hurt you," I say as I release him.

He chuckles. "Oh, so that's how it is?"

"Yep."

I make good progress on his ink. I finish most of the pool but that's because I work until eight. I clear away my things and Neymar walks me to my car after I lock up shop.

"You wanna come over to mine tomorrow night?" He opens my door.

Shit. I wasn't expecting that. "To yours?"

He smiles and I feel things. "Yeah, I always come you yours."

"Yeah, okay. That would be nice."

We smile stupidly at each other as I get into the car. He shuts the door but then opens it again and leans inside.

"Layla, I am sorry, for all this mess."

My smile slips and I sigh. "I know."

CHAPTER 16

I GET INTO WORK early on Tuesday and work straight through until four.

"Hey Hun, everything okay?" Johnny asks, appearing at my station.

"Yeah, all okay here." I continue wiping down my bench and think about seeing Neymar later.

This man has me thinking about him all damn day.

"Your last appointment just cancelled so you're done for the day."

"Really?" I'm shocked. *I never get cancellations...*

Johnny laughs. "Yep, family emergency, apparently." He wanders back to his desk so I decide to WhatsApp Neymar and see if he's free now.

–Hey. Wat u doin?–

He comes online and replies straight away.

–Nothing. How's work?–

–I've finished for the day, had a cancellation. Do you want to come in now?–

–How about you come link me for an hour first?–

Play hooky? I never skive off work... to hell with it.

–Love to.–

–I'll be there in five.–

–Okay.–

I smile wildly while I get my things together. I'm excited to see where Neymar lives. I tell the boys I'll be back later and once outside the front of the studio, I walk up two shops so that they don't see me getting into Neymar's car. It's not that I'm embarrassed by him, it's just not worth the million questions, especially from Maverick.

I see the Audi and wave him over to me and once I get inside, he pulls back into the slow moving traffic. It's always manic on this road *especially* at this time of day.

"Hey," I say nervously.

"Layla." He rests his hand on my thigh. "Good day?"

"So far."

He smirks. "I hope I can keep it that way."

"There's always room for improvement." We stop at a traffic light and he leans over and kisses me urgently. I bite my lip as he pulls away and a smile spreads across my face. "See, it's better already."

He bites his own lip. "Good."

The traffic clears and it's silent in the car for a while. It's not uncomfortable and I realise it's because our relationship is improving. We are definitely becoming more familiar with each other.

This is my chance...

"Do you know Maverick?" I ask him.

"Yeah, he used to run for me."

"Ohhh." I knew Maverick used to shot, that doesn't bother me.

"Why?"

"No reason."

"Don't lie to me."

I roll my eyes. "He just kinda warned me off a while ago, that's all."

"Ah, so that's why you were standing outside that bakery and not your studio."

Ugh, this man is so fucking aware. "You're quite observant, aren't you?"

"I have to be. Listen, that don't bother me, and I like that you asked me about Mav. The fact you're still here with me now, proves that you don't care about his opinion, so I'll allow it."

"You'll allow it?"

"Yeah."

"He works for me, and he's a good friend, I don't want no drama, I just wanted to know why he said what he said, that's all."

"He wanted out, he had to earn it, and that's as much as I've got to say about it."

I shrug. "Fine by me."

We arrive at Neymar's house and he holds my hand and walks me to his door. It's a three-storey townhouse with a black front door – no front garden. He opens the door and pulls me inside. When the door closes he pins me against it and kisses me again but more passionately this time. I press myself against him as his hands swarm my body and his tongue hungrily searches for mine. I moan against his mouth and the sound that escapes him is mind-numbing. *Oh god... I want him so bad.*

He releases me and we are both breathing hard. I watch him closely as he runs his hands over his head in frustration. We seem to have switched predicaments because now *he* is the one struggling with his 'no sex' condition.

"You okay?" I ask smugly.

"I will be soon, but you won't."

My stomach tightens at his words. I hope it won't be an empty threat. "I hope so," I reply unabashedly and I think I've shocked him by the look on his face.

He takes a deep breath and takes my hand in his. "Layla, Layla, Layla," he sighs, "You don't know what you're sayin'."

I can't tell you all the thoughts that are running through my head. All I know is that I would probably let him do just about anything he wanted to my body.

"I can imagine what you're thinking right now, just by that dirty look on your face." I look up to meet his gaze and blush. He takes me down the hall and into the kitchen. It's minimalist; black gloss units and white walls and floor. The units run all along the left wall and a table and chairs are under the window on the right.

"I made us dinner. If you're not hungry now, we can eat later."

"Actually, I am hungry so we can eat now. What did you cook?"

"Fried chicken." He releases my hand and after grabbing a glove, opens the oven and pulls out a dish. The chicken smells amazing and my stomach growls.

"Looks amazing."

"My secret recipe. There's dumpling in that container," he says pointing to a rectangular box on the side. "Take it to the table for me?"

"Sure." I do as he asked and he brings over the chicken and puts it down on a trivet. *Very domesticated...*

"Grape juice or Ciroc?"

"Grape juice. I still have to work and you shouldn't drink before getting a tattoo."

"Okay, boss." I hear him chuckle before he brings our drinks over to the table and sits down. He plates up my food and hands it to me. My mouth waters as I pick up a piece of chicken and take a bite. Damn, he's seasoned it perfectly. *My Mum would love him.*

"It's really good," I tell him, covering my mouth.

He looks pleased. "I'm glad you like it."

"I do. Who taught you how to cook?"

"My parents."

"Do they live here?"

He shakes his head. "Used to. They moved back to Trinidad when I was younger."

I knew there was an accent there. I watch him take a bite of a dumpling and then he licks his lips. I have to look away.

"How old are you?" I ask just to change my train of thought.

He's quiet for a moment and I look up. "How old do you think?"

I shrug. I'm guessing about the same age as me. "Twenty-eight?"

"Almost."

"Older?" I raise an eyebrow at him."

He shakes his head.

My eyes widen. "You're younger?"

"Yeah, twenty-seven."

Damn. "I would never have thought that."

He laughs and I scorn him. "What?"

"It's not funny."

"The look on your face was."

I roll my eyes and eat some of my dumpling. It's soft inside but crispy on the outside. I take another from the container. We eat mostly in silence after that. Neymar tells me that he's meeting with the owners of Entourage next week. I try and play it down for him but I know it's huge and he's feeling nervous. I'm happy for him, I know how hard it was for my brother to get out and I still shudder at the things he had to do to make that happen. I hope that Neymar doesn't have to do the same.

We head back to the studio at half five. I literally tag Johnny on the way out and get straight to work on Neymar's tattoo. It doesn't take me long to ink the rest of the pool and then I change needles before I start on the Wolf.

"So, it's Wolf time," I tell him.

He nods.

"You sure you still want it?" I bite my lip.

His eyes narrow. "Why wouldn't I?"

I shrug, "I dunno. Maybe because…" I pause. It feels like I'm putting my name on him. I know he loves my tattoo and he probably wouldn't be getting this Wolf on him if he hadn't seen mine. If things don't work out with us then he'll always be reminded of me.

"Because..?" he prompts, staring at me intently.

"Because, won't it always remind you of me?"

"Yeah."

"But what if things don't work out how you want them to?"

"I won't ever regret meeting you, Layla. Is that what you think?"

"I don't know. It feels so personal, and I always try and make people understand that although there *is* laser treatment, inking something like this on your skin is permanent y'know."

"I want the Wolf," he says, determined. "And I want you."

My heart stutters. Hearing him say that, in that way… I want him too, badly… but if he doesn't get this deal I don't know if I can be with him.

"What is it?"

I stare down at my machine in my hand. Honesty. He wants honesty from me. Tell him. "If you don't get that club–"

"Then, I'll look for something else."

"But you'll keep doing what you're doing and I don't want to run your life but I can't do it."

"I know, and I don't want you to. Can't you see that's why I'm trying not to hurt you? I want you close, but I'm also trying to keep you at arm's length."

He's right. He's keeping me hanging but he's not giving me empty promises. He's not even sleeping with me. "I know." I sigh heavily. He's trying to please everyone but something is going to have to give.

"You're worried?"

"Yes."

"What about?"

"About not being able to let you go, even if I should," I whisper.

There, I've said it.

I watch him while my words sink in. He nods and stares at the ceiling. He's so hard to read; my heart races as the silence continues.

"Once you finish this, maybe... you should take some time."

"Take some time?" Oh no... this is not what I wanted to hear.

"Stay away from me, and I'll stay away from you. I won't get involved if you want to date or... whatever. I want you to be sure, that it's me you really want."

I try to hide the hurt I feel at his words. I swallow hard and feel my heart breaking. *This is not what I wanted at all.* So, does he want me to go fuck other guys now, when he clearly told me he didn't want me to?

"Layla—"

"No, it's okay. I understand, I agree," I lie through my teeth. "Come, let me get this done then." I put my hand on his chest and press my foot back down. I'm gonna give him the best fucking tattoo he's ever seen.

CHAPTER 17

THE NEXT TIME Neymar comes into my studio it's awkward as hell. He's clearly being off with me, and I'm clearly pissed off at him. I feel like we should talk but none of us instigates it. I refuse when he asks to walk me to my car and even though I feel nervous about being on my own, I'm glad I have to. I need to get my life back on track and that means not being scared of being on my own again.

FRIDAY COMES and I think of Neymar often while I work. Today is his last session and quite possibly the last time I'll see him. Neymar and I won't cross paths out of work and I will make sure I go to great lengths not to see him.

I'm meeting the girls tonight so it's the perfect opportunity to start moving on from him. If Neymar really wanted me, he'd fight for me, which he clearly doesn't want to do. I know what it's like for these men in their gangs, it's their life. Their boys are their family, and no matter how much they think they might like a girl, she'll never come between that. I just feel angry that I let it go on for so long.

I'm so fucking dumb.

Neymar walks in, bang on six. I'm the only one left in the studio when he arrives so he walks straight over to my station.

"Layla," he says as he stands beside my chair.

Ugh. "Hey. You ready to finish this?" I choose my words wisely.

He nods before pulling off his shirt and it takes every bit of willpower I have not to admire his body. I focus on the ink so far and if I do say so myself, it's a masterpiece. Once the eyes and the shading on the wolf's neck is done, it's finished.

He lies down and after wiping his skin I get straight to it. Since Tuesday we haven't really spoken. It's just business now.

"You meeting the girls tonight?" he asks about half an hour later.

"Yep," I reply shortly.

He sighs and I glance at his face and he nods slowly. I wonder what's going through his mind right now. I'd love to spend just a minute inside there.

"You have any plans for the weekend?" I ask him, trying to be polite.

"No."

I nod my head but don't say anything. I'm sure he does have plans but like he told me before... he doesn't tell me things. *You can't live that life again, Layla. This is why you need to leave it alone...*

I change needles and work on the eyes. I feel him flinch a few times as I press the ink into his skin. The white shade hurts the most I think, but against his dark skin, it really takes it to the next level.

"All done," I tell him, trying to sound nonchalant. Inside I'm dying, no more Neymar time. I wipe his skin and hand him a mirror. He takes it from me as he sits up and moves his neck so that he can get a proper view of it all together. "It's amazing."

I smile but quickly wipe it from my face. "Some of my best work yet. Can I take a picture for my portfolio?"

"Yeah."

I grab the camera from my drawer and stand in front of him to get a good angle. I hear him breathing in the silence. His eyes are on me, I can feel them like his touch on my skin. I take a few pictures and then put the camera down on my desk. Once I clean his skin, I wrap him up then turn away and busy myself by clearing away my things.

"How much do I owe you?" he asks while zipping up his jacket.

"Eight-hundred." I know he said he'll pay double, but I just want what I'm owed.

"I'll get Jay to drop it over to you, if that's alright?"

"Of course." *I'm not evil.* He hovers while I'm cleaning. I know he wants to say something but I don't prompt him. He's a big man; if he has something to say, then he needs to just say it.

I hear him sigh which makes me turn to him. "I'll see you, then?" he says quietly. His tone stabs at me.

I nod. "I'll see you."

We stare at each other for a moment but then he turns and leaves. I hear the door close and it's like someone has flicked a switch on my emotions. Tears silently stream down my face as I throw the used needles into the sharps container. I put my machine away and have to stop several times to wipe my face. My chest feels so tight, I hurt—really hurt but I'm lucky to have gotten out now. If I feel like this after just a few weeks, I can't imagine what I'd feel like after longer... after being intimate with him.

I cry all the way home, in the car, in the bath, doing my hair and several times while doing my makeup which has made me really fucking late meeting the girls. The only good thing is that my face is almost back to normal, so I only had to apply a little bit of foundation. I check my face while in the taxi and see that my eyes aren't too puffy which is a miracle in itself.

The girls wave me over as I walk into the grill. I wave curtly and walk straight up to the bar and ask George for a double Henney with no chase. The girls look at me and then amongst themselves before Eve picks up the courage to say something to me.

"Babe, what's going on?" I hear the caution in her voice.

I down my drink and it burns the hell out of my throat. "Neymar. We've kinda decided not to see each other any more. George, I'll have another of those, thanks."

"Coming right up," he says with a beaming smile.

"Oh, babe, I'm sorry."

"Don't. Please," I say while holding up my hand. "*Please,* don't." My eyes well up and I take a deep breath, trying not to let the tears escape.

"I'm pregnant," Kelly says, abruptly.

Kara and Eve scream excitedly, drawing the attention of almost everyone in the bar. They hug her tightly and Kelly winks at me. *I'm so grateful for her right now.* I pretend not to know and congratulate her.

We talk about babies for the next two hours before Kelly heads home and Kara, Eve and I, make our way to Club Dorada across the street. I'm tipsy already and it's only eleven. The drinks keep going down in the club. Eve is a pro at getting guys to buy us drinks so I don't spend a penny of my own money.

We meet a group of guys who keep up our supply of drinks. One of them, Joel, asks me to dance so I say yes. We head through the crowd of people to the dance floor and start to dance. He's got good rhythm and I quickly get lost in the music. His hands are on my hips but I can't help but think about Neymar. I hate that he's in my mind so I kiss Joel. It's clumsy and he tastes of cigarettes and vodka.

I pull away and gag.

I'm gonna be sick.

I leave him on the dance floor and run to the girl's toilets. *Thank God there isn't a queue...* Once I lock myself in a cubicle, I try to throw up but I can't. I lean back against the toilet door with my eyes closed and tears threaten again... I take my phone out and scroll through my contacts to Neymar. My thumb hovers over the green phone symbol... I know he'd come now if I called him...

I'm playing with fire...

I can't do this. I press the back button and lock my phone screen.

"Layla, you in here, babe?" I hear Kara.

"I'm in here," I answer and then open the door. Eve and Kara look at me sympathetically. "I just wanna go home," I sob.

"We'll come with you," Eve says and then they hug me.

INSTEAD OF GOING HOME, I stayed the night at Eve's. I couldn't bear to be on my own. I was feeling too emotionally unstable, even more so after having a drink. I slept until five, and after avoiding Eve's interrogation, I'm finally in a taxi on my way home. I pay the driver and get out of the taxi before dragging myself to my front door. When I step inside, I kick a pale-brown envelope across my hallway.

My money from Neymar.

I drop my stuff on the side table and pick up the envelope. It's heavy. I open it up and slide out a wrapped stack of twenty-pound notes. This is way too much money and anger ignites inside me. I told him eight hundred, yet he's completely ignored me and given me more.

I hate him.

I go to the kitchen and after turning on the light, snap the elastic band and count out the money.

Three grand?

I swipe it angrily off the table and start crying, but I think it's more from anger now. I really want to text him and cuss him out but I know he'll try talk me down and I don't want that.

I'll take it back to him.

I pick the money up off the floor, put my eight-hundred into a jar in my cupboard, and then wrap up the rest with a pink elastic band from my drawer before shoving it back inside the envelope.

When I get to Neymar's house it's blacked out with no signs of anyone being at home. It's dark and no lights are on. I can't see the Range or the Audi either, so I leave the car running while I post the money through his door. I'm back at mine in twenty minutes and when I get in, I head straight for bed and cry myself to sleep.

I DON'T VISIT MY DAD ON SUNDAY. I feel guilty because I know he's disappointed, but I tell him I'm busy with work.

More lies.

I drag myself downstairs around lunchtime to make a tea but curse when I see there's hardly any milk, so reluctantly, I tie my hair up into a messy bun, pull on a hoody, grab my keys and run up to the shop on the corner. I walk back home with my head down and my hood up. I feel so fucking depressed, even though I know it's best to stay away from Neymar. It's just, I feel like someone has stolen my daylight because all I feel and see is darkness.

I walk through my front door and the same envelope is back. *Why the fuck is he doing this?*

I pull out my phone.

-I don't want this money.-

He comes online straight away and starts typing.

-It's wat I owe u.-

-I said 800!-

-I said I wld pay 3x-
-I don't want ur money!-
He doesn't reply.
Ugh.
Fuck him.
Prick.
It puts me in even more of a bad mood for the rest of the day and I don't answer anyone's calls or reply to any messages.
I'm not keeping that money.

I'M IN A FOUL MOOD when I get to work on Monday.
I don't want to be here.
Johnny brings me my coffee and I only just manage to mumble a thank you.

I miss Neymar so much, but I know he's bad for me, too. I know I can't go back to that life. I was always worried about my brother. Dante would come home with gunshot wounds, and he got stabbed a few times. I'd look after him and we would hide them from mum. When I think of those times, I know deep down I can't do it again. It doesn't make me feel any more happy about my situation, though.

My day is busy and I'm grateful. I take any drop-ins and piecing appointments I can get, just so I don't have to answer questions from the boys. I feel like I'm walking around with a constant black cloud over my head.

I lock up at seven and feel sad that everything is back to normal now. Ten 'til seven, Monday to Friday. I need to speak to Johnny tomorrow about changing my appointments back to nine 'til six. I've been getting up on time for a while now, so I might as well stick to starting at nine.

TUESDAY, AND WORK IS QUIETER. My mood hasn't improved one bit. When I close my eyes, I see his face. I feel his hands on my skin—his lips on mine. I'm tormenting myself with memories of him but I can't stop.

I sit on my stool and scroll mindlessly through Facebook. My next appointment is in half an hour, at two. I should eat really but I can't be bothered.

"Layla, are you okay? We're worried about you," Maverick says tentatively, sitting on my chair. I feel irritated because I've just fucking sterilised that.

"I'm fine."

"You don't look fine."

I narrow my eyes at him. "So you're saying I look like shit, then?"

"I didn't say that," he says defensively. "What is *wrong* with you?"

"I said nothing, alright."

He looks as though he's going to leave it but then changes his mind. "Is this about Jackson?"

"Don't say that name around me, okay?" I warn. *I do not want to be any more reminded of him.*

He flinches. "Okay, okay, I'm sorry, just know that we're all here for you, okay?"

"Sure." *Even though I bet you'd be really fucking happy considering you told me to stay away from him.*

He walks away and I feel relieved. Seriously, I just want to be left the hell alone. I don't know how many times I have to say the same shit over and over again.

I POST THE MONEY BACK TO NEYMAR AFTER WORK. If it gets lost in the post—even better. I just don't want it. Eve calls me when I get home to tell me she's broken up with her new guy, so we're going clubbing Friday night. I'm just excited to get drunk. That's all I seem to ever do these days; work, drink, cry and sleep.

My new dresses have arrived from my dressmaker, though, and there's a really inappropriate one I want to wear. I've even ordered shoes online to match it. Deep down I know I seem to be spiralling, but I can't seem to find a way out.

I wish I never got involved with Neymar.

I hate him so much.

CHAPTER 18: NEYMAR

"I FUCKING TOLD YOU, I'm not on that, you deaf or what?"

"It's an easy in and out ting, Jackson. Ten minutes, tops."

I hang up the phone and Jay stares at me. "What?"

"Nothing."

"That's what I thought." I read through my messages. Still no word from Layla. I read the last message she sent me. She wouldn't take the money, even though it was what we agreed.

Why?

I shove my phone in my pocket and ignore it when it rings again. I stare out the window and feel my mood drop further. I feel like shit; I have since I left her studio. I said she should take some time so she didn't feel pressured to be with me, but I still thought she would make the decision to link me. She knew I was switching what I did, I practically fucking told her I was doing it to be with her.

My phone rings again and I check it this time. Kimani. "What?"

"It's clean. Does that mean you're out now?"

"It will be if I sort out that ting later. You and Jay need to decide what you're doin'."

"What about the man dem, you going to tie up those loose ends before you chip?"

"I said I fucking was, don't think I'm goin' soft just because I'm getting out."

"Chill, boss, I never said that."

I hang up and look back out the window.

"Seriously, bruv, I love you, but you need to sort your shit out."

Fuck off, Jay. "I am."

"Then you need to sort things out with Layla."

My anger peaks. "Don't talk to me about her."

"I fucking will."

I turn to face him. *I will kill you.*

"Don't look at me like that. You've been a headache ever since you let her go."

"I said," I say, looking back outside, "I don't want to–" *That's her friend, Eve.* "Pull over."

"What?"

I glare at him. "Pull. Over. Now."

He does as he's told and I roll down my window to wait for Eve to pass. "Eve!"

She looks around before clocking us and then smiles as she walks over. "Hey, you two." I watch her check out Jay as she leans in the Range window. Her pupils dilate and she bites her bottom lip. She likes him, a lot. "What you guys up to?"

"How's Layla?" I ask, blunt as fuck. Fuck it, I want to know.

She looks at me and frowns. "I'd say just as good as you."

Not good then. This is good, but why ain't she called?

She looks back at Jay. "Jay, looking fucking *hot*. Still got that girlfriend?"

"Actually, no," he replies and I glance at them both. They're grinning at each other. It pisses me off.

"Why hasn't she called me, then?" I interrupt.

She shrugs and shakes her head. "I don't know. She won't talk to anyone. I just know that she looks like shit and feels even worse. Her mood is atrocious."

"So is his," Jay comments and I narrow my eyes at him.

"Look, I don't know if she told you, but I've been tryin' to buy Entourage and–"

"*You* are buying Entourage?" She's surprised.

Whatever.

"Maybe. I was doing some shit before, but I thought she'd be happy that I was moving past that."

"She never told me that, but like I said, she's shut everyone out. She hardly even answers her phone anymore. You two just need to get together already because this shit is getting old. I want my friend back." Her attention quickly refocuses on Jay. "So, no more girlfriend?"

"No."

"You want an upgraded one?"

I look at Jay and he's grinning. "Maybe."

Her eyes light up at that. "Take my number." She reads it out and my thoughts return to Layla. Why is she staying away if she feels as bad as I do? I don't get it.

I check the time. "We need to go."

"Okay, nice to see you both. Jay, don't make me wait, yeah?"

"I won't."

She gives me a nod. "See you later, Jackson."

I watch her walk away and I wonder if she'll tell Layla she's seen us.

"We're gonna be late, you need to hurry up," I tell Jay.

"I will."

I feel unusually nervous as we approach the club. I need to get this. I need it—to get her. At least if I can sign these deeds, I can move to her again with something different to offer. Fucking woman has me on some next level shit.

"Looks like you're both unhappy. I told you she looks rough."

"Shut the fuck up." She couldn't look rough if she tried, she's way too sexy. I want her so fuckin' bad.

"Sorry, but you know what I mean."

"Find out from Eve if they're going out tomorrow night. Don't be bait though, Jay."

"I won't. I'll text her in a bit."

My mood lifts. If all goes to plan here, I can find her tomorrow. I wonder if she'll talk to me? The thought of her not wanting to, hurts.

CHAPTER 19

I GET HOME from work on Thursday evening and go straight to the kitchen to make a tea. I'm not even gonna bother cooking. God knows the last time I ate a proper meal.

I hear banging on my door and turn to look through the hallway at the smoked glass. *Eve?*

I let her in and close the door. "What are you doing here?" I try not to sound rude but fail.

She raises the plastic bag in her hand. "I bought barbecue and thought we could talk?"

I roll my eyes. "I don't want to." I smell the barbecue and my stomach growls.

"Yes, you do. You haven't spoken to any of us and you need to. Look at you."

"What?"

She drops the bag on my hallway table and stands behind me, guiding me to the mirror. "*That.* Bags under your pretty brown eyes... frown lines and look at your cheeks... you are looking so gaunt in the face, Layla."

I step out of her hold and walk to the kitchen. I don't want to talk about how shit I feel. Tears pool in my eyes while I finish making my tea. Eve grabs some plates and cutlery and sets the table for us to eat.

"I'm not hungry."

"Yes, you are."

"I'm not."

"Girl, I am not leaving here until you talk to me, so it's up to you how long I'm here for."

I get annoyed. "You've just broken up with your man, why do you wanna hear about *my* shit?"

She's quiet for a moment. "Because, I wasn't in love."

I snort. "I am not in love with Neymar."

She drags a chair out from under the table and narrows her eyes at me. "At least be honest to yourself, even if you aren't with anyone else."

"I'm..." Is this what this is? Is this why I feel so fucking hopeless?

"Come on, eat with me." Her voice is gentle this time, encouraging.

I sigh heavily and sit down with my tea. She dishes out my favourite food, ribs and brisket with salad. Tears threaten again. She knows me so well. "Thank you."

She smiles and hands me a fork. I take it and she picks up hers. She stabs a bit of her salad and then looks at me. "Talk to me, babe."

I watch her eat and it makes me feel hungry. I pick up a rib and bite into it. God, it tastes so good, I think I moan. Eve coughs and after I swallow my mouthful, I take a deep breath.

"Eve, I just, I feel so... *low*. I'm so miserable." My body jerks as I sob and then I'm crying. She's up from the table and holding me around my shoulders as tears stream down my face and onto my leggings. "I know it's for the best, but I feel like I *need* him."

She rubs my back and hushes me comfortingly. "I know, Hun."

I wipe my face and calm myself so I can talk. It feels good to have said that aloud. Eve sits back down and I decide to let it all out. "He said we should stay away from each other, so I can make sure he's what I want."

"Clearly he is, because look at you without him."

"But he lives a lifestyle that I can't get involved with again. He's into some dark shit, Eve. You know what it was like with Dante. I can't go back to worrying about someone like that."

"But he's trying to get out of that life, isn't he?"

I frown. "How do you know about that?"

She looks nervous.

"How do you know, Eve?"

"I saw them, Jackson and Jay, earlier today."

"Where?"

"Central, after work. They pulled over to talk to me."

Oh my God, she saw him. "What did they say?"

"Jackson asked how you were, he looks as shit as you by the way. Moody, too."

I feel good after hearing that. He must miss me too.

She sighs. "You clearly miss each other. I think you're both being stupid."

"It's not that simple, Eve. I told you, that life isn't for me."

"But if he's getting out-"

"But what if he doesn't? How will I know he can truly leave that life behind?"

"Well, for one, you won't know unless you talk to him and two, how long are you going to keep on living like this then?"

I bite my lip. "I don't know."

"I think you should call him."

"No."

"Yes."

"No, Eve." I eat some brisket and feel her staring at me but ignore her. I can't call him. I need to move on. I can get over this, I just need more time.

"At least think about it, okay?"

Why is she on his side all of a sudden? "I will."

We eat the rest of our food and I make her a drink.

"Are we going out tomorrow night?" she asks as I hand her a glass of juice.

"Yeah. Is Kara coming?"

She rolls her eyes. "No. She's all settling down and shit."

"Just the two of us, then?"

"Yep. I'll get us on a guestlist somewhere."

"Can we just have a good time," I ask her, feeling slightly better after our talk. "Just the two of us, no men?"

"Definitely."

I slump in my chair and feel thankful she came over. "I love you, Eve."

She gives me a sympathetic smile. "I love you too, girl."

WORK DRAGS, but the thought of getting drunk tonight helps me get through it. I pack up my things and leave the studio. I start at nine now and it's nice to be home by half six. I take a long soak in the bath and do the usual girl stuff before a night out. I straighten my hair and put some curls in the ends with my tongs and then choose what I'm going to wear.

I pick out the new dress. It's outrageous, sky blue and covers my ass and tits and that's basically it. It's a halter neck so no back, and it has cut-outs all up my right side. I match it with my new silver heels and a sparkly clutch bag. I feel amazing when I look in the mirror, especially as I can finally ditch the foundation and put my natural face back on display again.

I get a taxi to Eve's and wait for her to come out. She soon appears at her door and hurries down the steps to me. She's wearing a red cropped top and an obscenely short bandage skirt with black stilettos.

"You look hot as fuck," I tell her when she gets inside.

"Thanks, babe." She looks over what I'm wearing and smiles hard. "That colour is popping on you, Hun, we will have to fight the boys off us tonight."

"You know that." I smile, and it feels like I haven't for so long. It feels good.

Eve got us on the guest list for WonderLounge which is a favourite of ours. It has six different rooms so you can dance to anything you want. We usually jump between Afrobeats and Club Classics.

We get a lot of appreciative looks as we walk up to the bar but I know it's because we look hot as hell tonight. I order us a bottle of champagne, feeling the need to celebrate turning a corner in my depression. A hand taps me on my shoulder as I pour our drinks and I turn to see a sexy guy with dark hair and dark eyes looking over my body. His eyes meet mine and he smiles devilishly.

"I'm Derrick."

"Nice to meet you, Derrick, but I'm not doing guys tonight," I tell him with a smirk. He's hot, I can't lie. He makes a mock sad face and it makes me smile again. "Shame I didn't meet you on another night."

"It is. See you around?" He's hopeful.

"I hope so." I watch him walk into the crowd and disappear before turning back around to Eve.

"What was that about?" she asks curiously.

I smile. "Some guy. Don't worry, I told him, no men allowed."

She looks around and then back to me. "Good."

We draw the attention of a few more guys at the bar before heading to the Club Classics room. I soon finish my drink and pour us both another glass before leaving the empty bottle next to a wall. I close my eyes as I sip it, letting the alcohol and the music hit me. Music understands me, the right song can always cheer me up.

I'm feeling the best I have in ages and while I rock my hips to the music, I feel more and more happy inside. I feel tipsy already, though, and wish I had of eaten something before I came out. I shout into Eve's ear that I'm going to the toilet but she stays to enjoy her favourite song; *Chingy, One call away.*

While I'm in the toilets, I reapply my lip gloss and wipe away the smudged eyeliner from under my eyes. I notice my face looks extra skinny in these mirrors. *I need to eat.*

I make my way back to Eve. Pushing through the people on the dance floor, I finally find her dancing with a guy... who looks suspiciously like... *Jay?*

I walk up to them and pull Jay's shoulder to turn him around.

He looks surprised. "Layla?"

I look at Eve. "What the fuck are you doing?"

"We're just dancing, Layla, calm down," she shouts over the music.

I ignore her and turn my attention back to Jay. "I thought you had a girlfriend?"

"Not any more. Look Layla–"

"Oh my God," dread fills me. "Is he here?" *Please say no...*

He nods.

Fuck. "I'm leaving."

"Layla, wait, I'll come with you," Eve shouts and grabs my arm. "I'm sorry."

"I can't see him, Eve. I swear."

"Okay." She bites her lip nervously. "We'll go, right now, okay? Come on."

We leave Jay on the dance floor and make our way outside. It's cold and the alcohol clouds my mind. My heart hurts from how hard it's pounding. *I can't see him. I can't.*

Eve holds my hand firmly as we quickly walk around the corner to the taxi rank. I feel relieved when there are only two people in front of us.

"I'm sorry, babe, I wasn't thinking." She looks upset and I reassure her that I'm not mad at her.

"I don't care if you see Jay, okay, I like him. I just really can't see Neymar right now. I *can't...*" I try so hard to contain my emotions but I can't and tears fall. I know if I see him it will bring it all back. It's been almost two weeks and after the work Eve put in with me, if I saw him now... it would ruin it all.

It would destroy me.

Eve pulls me into a hug and I hold her tightly. She rubs my back but abruptly stops. "Oh, fuck, babe."

"What?" I ask, feeling anxious from the tone in her voice.

"It's Jackson."

I pull back; a hundred emotions flooding through me at once. *Oh God...* I panic, suddenly feeling sick.

Eve gasps. "Are you okay? You've gone really pale."

I'm shaking. "Where is he?" *I'm so scared of seeing him.*

"Across the road. He's just got out of a black car, he's coming over."

A taxi pulls up and the next person in the queue jumps in. *Fuck!* I watch her eyes following him.

"You look stunning, babe." She wipes under my eyes. "He's almost here. You can do this."

"I can't," I whisper.

"You can."

I watch her eyes and I know he's close. I take a steadying breath.

"Layla?" Neymar says my name and my body becomes the biggest traitor of all time and instantly answers his call. I watch Eve's eyes flicker between him and me and then he says my name again but this time with the extra meaning he always puts in.

I turn around and my breath catches; his hair is freshly faded and he's dressed in black pants and a shirt. *Ugh...* I'd forgotten just how fucking sexy he was. He looks at me with those beautiful eyes and I am so screwed. I feel myself wanting to close the gap between us and then the effect he has on me makes me mad.

"What do you want, Jackson?" I clutch my bag to my chest, needing something between us.

He looks wounded. "I need to talk to you."

"About what?" I try my hardest not to look at those lips but fail, again. I groan inwardly. Another taxi pulls up and the person in front of us gets in.

"Not here, okay? Come with us."

His gaze is too much and I have to look away.

"Please," he says, insisting. I look past him and see Jay waiting across the street with the Range window down, staring at us. *I need to say no, I need to stay away...*

"Layla-"

"Okay!" I snap. I hate when he says my name like that. "Come on, Eve."

We follow him across the street to the car and he opens the door to let me in. Eve jumps in the front and I scorn her for leaving me in the back with him. I slide over as far as I can get to the other side and he gets in behind me. My heart pounds. I smell his cologne and it stirs my memories of him. I curse myself for letting him get to me, again. *What am I doing?*

Eve starts chatting away with Jay in the front but the sound of my beating heart drowns them out. I know Neymar's staring at me, he makes me feel so fucking exposed. I stare mindlessly out the window and try to ignore it but I can't. I close my eyes and exhale deeply. *Get it together, Layla, please.*

"Layla?"

"What?" I answer Eve, calling my name. I feel so on edge.

"We're gonna go back to Jackson's, is that okay?"

"Fine," I snap, but I am glad Eve's here because at least I won't be on my own with *him.*

CHAPTER 20

WE GET TO Neymar's house and as usual, after he gets out, I follow. I quickly walk around him as he shuts the car door and walk with Eve. *Why did I agree to come here...?*

I shiver from the cold as I watch him open his front door. Eve and Jay are smiling wildly at each other, and I'm sure Jay taps her ass as they step inside. I hold my breath as I walk in.

Don't look at him...

I follow the others into the kitchen and we sit at the kitchen table while Jay opens a bottle of Ciroc Amaretto, the same one I drank at Entourage which brings back more memories... Neymar sits beside me and hands me a glass. I mutter *thanks* but don't look at him; I know what those eyes can do.

Jay and Eve are getting on really well and are openly flirting with each other. Eve loves a bad boy so I'm not surprised she's attracted to him. I feel so awkward here, compared to the first time I came. I watch how carefree Eve looks with Jay, but she doesn't know the half of what I went through with Dante... *I should warn her.*

"Let's go for a cigarette," Eve says to Jay. I look up and glare at her but she doesn't see. *Ugh...* Thanks a lot, Eve. *Fuck.*

I watch them leave us to go out the back to smoke. I know Neymar's gonna try and talk to me. I look down at my drink as my heart races.

"Layla–"

"What do you want, Jackson?" I ask blankly while swirling the Ciroc around in my glass.

"Don't call me that."

"Why not?" I snap back.

"Because I hate when you call me that."

"It's your name."

He sighs harshly. "Please don't be like this."

"Like what?" I look up at him but regret it. His brown eyes catch me off guard and I am instantly drawn in.

"Like this." He looks like he's hurting but he's the one who said he wanted a break.

"You said we should take a break from each other, we have nothing more to talk about." I look back down at my drink.

"That's not what I said."

I sigh. "That's not how I remember it."

"I miss you..."

He may as well have just killed me with those words. I close my eyes briefly...

Don't let him do this to you again...

"...And I know you've missed me, too." My eyes find his again and the look on his face tells me he means it. God, I have missed him.

"I can't do this," I whisper painfully.

"Please, Layla."

I bite my lip and close my eyes. "I..."

I hear Eve and Jay coming back in from outside and after downing my drink, focus on them.

"Babe?" Eve says while walking over to us. "Do you mind if I go to Jay's?" She looks at me nervously and I know she's really asking if it's okay to leave me here with Neymar. I can feel him staring at me.

"Now?" I can't hide my panic. We've only just got here.

"Yeah."

Fuck sake... I look at Jay and then back to Eve. I can't cock-block her. I rub my fingers on my temples in torment. "That's fine," I tell her defeated. I know I should say no but clearly being burnt a few times already is not enough for me.

"You sure, yeah?" Her voice is quieter this time but I answer the same.

"Call me tomorrow?"

"I will."

She kisses me on the cheek and then grabs her coat off her chair. "Nice to see you again, Jackson."

"You too," he replies but I don't feel as though he's looked away from me.

"See ya, Layla," Jay says cautiously before leaving with Eve. The door closes and my heart races. I feel so vulnerable now it's just him and me.

"Do you want another drink?" he offers quietly.

"Just a little bit," I answer, sliding my glass over to him. I haven't eaten so my tolerance is low.

He pours the Ciroc in my glass and stops after about an inch. I hear him pour himself a glass and then drink some before putting it back down on the table.

"I think about you all the time, I can't get you out my head. I hate everyone and everything, without you."

Oh, God... I know what he means. I have been the biggest bitch since we stopped talking. "But you said we should stay away from each other," I mutter.

"I wanted you to make a decision about us. To decide if I was what you really wanted."

"You were what I wanted and I thought I was the one who always made that clear." I want to look at him but I don't.

"But not now?"

I face him but the look he gives me breaks my heart. I look back into my glass... I still want him now. He's saying all the right things and I'm struggling to stay mad at him. *God*, why do I like him so much, *why...*

"Say something, anything."

"I don't know what you want me to say."

"Tell me you still want me... tell me you've missed me." I can hear the pain in his voice.

I take a drink from my glass and then get lost in his eyes. "I do and I have." Relief spreads across his face and it strangely makes me feel good inside. He smiles and I can't help but smile back at him. I have missed those lips and to be honest, it feels good being around him again.

He frowns. "You look slim."

"I know," I say quietly and bite my lip.

"You hungry?" he asks before getting up from the table. I watch him walk over to the fridge and take out a white container. "I have some fried chicken."

I should eat. "Yeah, that would be good."

He gets out some plates and cutlery and puts them on the side.

"I need to use the bathroom."

"You know where it is," he says as I get up from the table. I see his eyes find my tattoo. I wish he would touch it again. My mind is already running wild with thoughts, and when I reach the bathroom, I shut the door with a tormented sigh. I wonder if his deal went through and that's why he's brought me here? If he thinks he can fuck me now... *Ugh...* he's right.

I adjust my breasts in my bra and realign my dress so that the slits line up with my tattoo. I run my fingers through my hair and then return to the kitchen. He's dishing out the food but stops when I walk back in. Our eyes meet and instead of walking back to my seat, I'm drawn towards him. He puts the fork he's holding down on the side and steps towards me, looking over my body as I approach him.

We stand in front of each other in silence. *I want him so badly.* Seeing him again has made me realise that no matter how hard I try to hate him, I don't want to be without him. He swallows hard and then blindly hands me a plate.

Are you fucking serious? I'm basically handing myself to him on a silver-fucking-platter, and he offers me food, *not* sex? I roll my eyes and walk back over to the table. I feel my body shaking in anger. Why the fuck did I let him do this to me again? Why did I think that this time would be any different from all the others?

I down my drink and snatch up my bag. "Goodbye, Jackson." I practically spit his name out and walk angrily out of the kitchen.

He reaches for my arm. "Layl–"

I pull myself from his grip and glare at him. "Don't fucking touch me!"

"What is wrong with you?" He looks confused and it only makes me angrier

"What's wrong with *me*?" I scoff and turn from him. I walk quickly to his front door, but before I can open it, his hand presses it shut from above me.

"Let me fucking leave," I seethe. I need to get out of here. I feel so angry. I am so fucking gullible that I actually just fell for the same shit.

"No."

I turn around to face him. "I fucking *hate* you!" The words spill my mouth but even as I say them, I know they aren't true. His glare intensifies and I have to turn back to face the door.

"Is that what you've been telling yourself?" He sounds surprised.

"I haven't been telling myself anything. I just know, I hate you. Open the door." I stand with my arms crossed and feel him move closer. I feel the heat of his body behind mine and want him again.

Damn it.

"You don't hate me. Far from." His breath is hot on the back of my neck. It makes me close my eyes, just so I can concentrate enough to breathe.

"I do." *Please, just give me what I want.*

"You don't." I feel his lips on my skin and I know he hears my sharp intake of breath. "Just tell me why you're so mad with me?"

"Please, I can't take this shit no more," I say desperately. "Just let me go."

His hand slips into one of the slits in my dress and then grabs my hip, pulling me roughly back against him. I feel his hardness and bite my lip to stifle a moan. *Don't give him the satisfaction.*

"Do you want me to fuck you now?"

I feel every word, not just on my neck but in my crotch, too. *Oh God... yes.* "No."

"Don't lie to me, Layla." His hand slips around my naked stomach and then lower.

"I don't..." I whisper. *Just a little lower...*

"Liar. Tell me what you want."

"To leave." I'm barely breathing now. All I can think about is how good his hand feels on my skin... His fingers brush lightly between my legs but I feel it so damn hard. I rest my forehead on the door. "*Please.*"

"Tell me what you want and I promise, I'll give it to you."

His fingers slip inside my thong and I gasp. "I want..."

"What, Layla?"

"You in me."

He spins me around and with one swift movement, his hand is up my dress and between my legs. I drop my bag on the floor. "Fuck," I whimper as his skin touches mine.

He leans in close with his eyes closed. "Do you know how fucking bad I want you?"

I bite his lip hard and he groans before pushing me back against the door. His lips press to mine and he kisses me hungrily. My world stops and I push closer to him as my hands find his back to pull him against me. He picks me up easily but doesn't take his mouth from mine. I wrap my arms and legs around him as he carries me upstairs.

He drops me down on the bed and then covers me with his body, resting on his hands either side of me while I eagerly reach for the buttons on his shirt...

I'm under him... finally...

I watch him, watching me, breathing heavily, my mind is lost and all I can think about is getting him inside me. His hard body comes into view and I sigh as I run my hands over his perfectly, defined muscles. I bite my lip, he's so fucking sexy I can't handle it. My gaze settles on my artwork and I feel a flutter inside, remembering our sessions together.

He gets up and shrugs off his shirt and then pulls me to sit up and grabs the back of my dress to pull it up from under me. He roughly pulls it over my head and then reaching behind me, he unsnaps my bra and I move my arms to help him take it off. I throw it beside us and try to calm the fuck down.

He lets out a low groan as he appreciates me in just my thong and then watches me as I unbuckle his gold belt and pop open his fly. He reaches into his pocket and pulls out a condom. I frown. *Had he planned to fuck me this whole time?*

"The answer is yes."

"How do–"

"Do you want this?" he asks, using his beautiful eyes to silence me.

I press my hand firmly against his hardness and watch as his face screws up. "You are not saying no to me again, Neymar, I swear to God," I warn.

He shakes his head. "I fucking ain't." He removes his jeans and boxers and my eyes find his length and my insides clench. This is the closest I've been to getting what I want and I'm so scared that he's going to change his mind again... I reach to touch him but he catches my wrist and pins me back down on the bed and rests beside me. His hands are quickly back on my body, making my skin burn. He caresses me everywhere, squeezing my thighs and then sliding his hands up my hips to my waist.

He pulls my thong and rips it, so I lift my hips for him to slide it out from under me. His fingers slip confidently between my legs and I gasp. He strokes from my clit, down, until a finger slips inside me.

"Oh, God," I moan as my hips jerk against his touch. His eyes bore intensely into mine and my heart flutters. He watches me with parted lips while pushing another finger inside my wetness. I'm so turned on my body feels like it will snap any second. I'm so ready for him; I've never been so aroused in my life. His fingers swirl purposely inside me and I almost sob, it feels so good.

I want to close my eyes but he's looking at me in such a way that I can't... He's touching me and it hurts... *I've wanted him for so long.* He shifts his hand and presses it against my swollen flesh making me moan again and bite my lip.

"Shit, Layla, you are the sexiest fucking woman I've ever known." He groans and snatches his fingers away to reach beside him for the condom. My insides quiver as he rips it open and I watch as he rolls it down onto his cock. It's thick, hard and my insides jump from the sight of it. I just can't take my eyes off it. I would suck him so good, and I'm not really one for oral sex... *I'd even let him bust in my mouth...*

I feel his hand on my chin and I look him in the eyes. "Don't look at it like that, Layla, damn!" He climbs over me and I hold on to his shoulders while he positions himself between my legs so he's right... *there.*

He kisses me softly as I tighten in protest while he fills me. We both moan as he reaches my end. The sound that comes out of me is like a cry and he promptly gives me a look as if he's asking permission to carry on.

I nod, but I'm so overwhelmed. *I had started to think that this would never happen.* I rock my hips up against him and take him all with a whimper. I close my eyes and breathe; my mind can't focus on even the basics right now.

He moans as he pulls back and then slowly buries himself back inside me. "Do you hate me now?" he whispers before resting his forehead against mine.

"Yes."

He thrusts harder at my reply and I gasp. *"I hate you, so much."*

"There ain't no going back now," he says darkly and pushes a hand under my ass. I hold him around the base of his neck and he closes his eyes while he pulls me against him. I feel every single inch of him, filling me so well. I tighten around him and the sound that he makes excites me madly. He picks up the pace and although he's too much for me to take, it still feels like he's giving me the best fuck of my life.

He takes his hand from under me and finds my aching breasts. He pinches my nipples and I close my eyes... I feel like crying, it's too much... too intense. He grips my hip and pulls me up. I cry out when he reaches my limit but at the same time, fire ignites inside me.

"Fuck this," he groans and flips me over onto all fours. He wastes no time in entering me again and then pulls me up so my back is against his front. He starts long hard strokes inside me while he squeezes my breasts and kisses my neck.

I moan his name through my heavy panting... "Neymar..." *Oh God...* His name sounds like a plea as it falls from my lips.

"Layla," he replies, "Fuck, you feel so good." His thrusts quickly become more urgent, harder slams. I dig my nails into his arm as a release. It's too good, *so good...* The sounds he makes are so fucking erotic that I feel the ignition of my orgasm and I quickly become lost as my body begins to shake; my hips frantically rocking against his, the feeling so intense that I have to lean back onto his body as the waves relentlessly crash through my body.

He calls my name and holds me tightly while he comes. I feel him release and then his body stills and he buries his head in the curve of my neck. I can feel his harsh breath on my skin and his heart pounding against my back. I gently stroke his arm and he moans softly making my heart stutter.

I am *so* ruined.

He pulls out and slowly lowers me to the bed. I lie on my belly and realise that I'm sore, but finally, well and truly satisfied.

He moves my hair from the side of my face and lies beside me. "Don't stay away from me again, Layla. I can't take it."

My chest constricts at his words and I know that I won't be able to. "I won't."

He kisses my cheek and then gets up from the bed. I roll over and watch him slip off the condom and then leave to dispose of it. I sigh deeply and close my eyes. I know I'm in love with him, but I also know I'm playing a very dangerous game with my heart. His life is a mess and even if he did manage to get that deal, his roots will always haunt him. I'd be stupid to think that he could ever leave that life entirely behind, no matter how much he tries, or wants to.

I get up to find my bra and put it on. He returns and hands me a black t-shirt. "Wear this if you want." He's wearing a pair of black boxers but he's still quite obviously hard. He looks over my body as he sits on the edge of his bed. "You gonna eat, now?"

"Yeah."

He suddenly looks anxious. "Do you regret it?"

I shake my head. "No, why would you think that?"

"You're so quiet."

"I'm just, overwhelmed," I answer honestly. *That was so good...* "It was... amazing."

He looks deep in thought. "It was."

"That's why you wanted to wait," I say as realisation hits. *How did he know it would be so good?*

"That's why I *had* to wait. I could barely stay away from you before," he sighs, "I won't be able to at all now. I need you in my life. I want you to be *my* woman. Thinking about you with someone else makes me fucking crazy, Layla. When I said you should take some time, I never thought you would actually stay away."

"I didn't want to..." I *had* to, but now I'm not going to be able to stay away from him anymore and the feeling worries me. "Neymar, I like you, a lot–"

He laughs. "You think we *like* each other?"

I'm rocked by his knowing look. *He loves me, too?*

"Come on, you need to eat."

HE REHEATS THE CHICKEN and we sit at the table to eat. It's four in the morning and after we finish eating, I start feeling tired. He clears our glasses and plates, loading them into the dishwasher.

"Do you want some help?"

"Nah, I'm good. You wanna sleep?"

I yawn as if right on queue. "I don't mind."

"I bought Entourage." He turns to look at me and I smile.

So he did it, he actually bought it. "Congratulations," I say happily. "I know it was important to you."

He smiles "You don't know how much."

"So, does that mean that me and my girls are on the guest list now?"

He laughs. "That's all you have to say?"

"I said congratulations first."

"You're funny."

"Seriously, though, I'm really happy for you." *And me.* I'm desperately trying to play it cool.

He gives me a suspicious glance. "Don't you mean you're happy for *us*?" I see him smiling as he puts the last dish into the dishwasher.

"Maybe that, too."

He closes the door and starts the cycle. I watch him run a glass of water and take a packet of tablets from his cupboard.

"Here," he says, bringing them to me.

How did he know? I pop two paracetamol and down the water. I put the glass down and he looks at his t-shirt on me.

"Come here," he demands. I get up from my chair and walk around the table to him. He turns me to my side and runs his hand up my tattoo. "This is sexy as fuck."

"I think you've told me that before," I say smiling.

He spins me and pulls me onto his lap. I straddle him and his hardness rubs against my thigh.

"Do you want to get some sleep?" I ask playfully.

"Fuck, sleep."

CHAPTER 21

I SMELL NEYMAR AS I WAKE. A hand slides over my ass and between my legs. I feel sore from all the sex but my body still greedily wants more.

"You hungry?" he asks softly, kissing me behind my ear.

Trying to feed me again. "Mmm," I reply and he pushes a finger inside me.

"Neymar." I can't tell if his name sounds like a warning or an invitation.

"I love it when you say my name."

He explores me and I moan. *He'll be the death of me.*

"Why don't you shower, and I'll make us breakfast?"

I hum and nod into the pillow and he moves away from me.

"I've left a towel in there. Don't fall back asleep, Layla. It's eleven, and I know you go and see your Mum on a Saturday."

I open my eyes. "Eleven?"

He's standing by the side of the bed, dressed already. He's wearing a white t-shirt and black jeans. "You look good."

He smiles. "So do you, but you need to get your ass up, sexy."

A smile spreads over my lips. I like that.

"I'm serious. Up." He walks out of the room and I stretch out under the covers. *Ugh...*

I shower and put my dress back on from last night. There's a toothbrush with the towel so I brush my teeth after washing my face. My hair's a mess but I manage to tame it with my fingers and some water, going for a to-the-side, wavy look. I find Neymar in the kitchen on his phone. He watches me as I walk in and motions for me to sit down.

"I said I wasn't on that, Jay.... you need to deal with that."

He pulls a tray out of the oven and places it on the stove. "I'm with her now..." he looks at me and then turns away. "It don't matter, I'm not getting involved in that shit. Tell Kimani to deal with it. They must think I'm fucking playing. I said, no." He presses a button on the coffee machine and it starts to make a whirring noise. I can see him getting angry by the way he starts to move around the kitchen. "Nah, fuck that, I'll call you later." He puts his phone on the side and brings over the tray with a cup. "People piss me off," he says harshly, handing me the tea.

"Work?" I ask.

"Drama." He sighs. "I made us eggs and plantain. That okay?"

"Yeah."

He collects his coffee from the machine and joins me at the table. "What time you going to your mum's?"

"I usually go at two and have dinner with her."

"So, I'll see you after?"

I can't help but smile. "Yeah, if you want."

He smiles, too. "I want. I have a new number as well so make sure you put it in your phone before I drop you home."

I look at my bag on the side of the table and nod. "Okay."

AFTER BREAKFAST, I replace Neymar's number and then he reluctantly drops me home. I get changed into a skirt and vest and then make my way to my mum's house.

"Mum?" I call out as I get inside.

"In here!" I follow her voice into the kitchen. "Mum, what are you doing?" I ask as I see her up on the worktop reaching for something in the cupboard. I move over to her. She's wearing a long skirt, so I worry she could slip any minute. She turns her head to face me and her brown skin creases at her forehead.

I panic. "Mum, get down, I'll get what you want."

I help her down and she goes over to the kettle. "You want tea?"

"Yes, Mum. What would you like out of here?" I ask while looking at what's on the shelves.

"The coconut cream."

I find it and shut the cupboard. She takes it from me and crumbles it into a pot of boiling water. "How have you been then, Mum?"

"Alright. Your face looks much better."

"I know."

"Try not to get hurt again." She gives me a look that I know all too well from growing up. She's strict and even though I'm grown, I still respect her.

"I won't, Mum."

She washes the rice for the pot and my thoughts drift to Neymar. I can't wait to see him again—I have it so bad. The way he handled my body last night has got me thinking all sorts of things. My phone buzzes in my bag and I check it.

It's him.

-I can't wait to fuck you... again.-

Oh God... Great minds think alike. *-I was just thinking the exact same thing.-*

"Who you messaging?"

I look up and Mum is staring at me. "No one, Mum."

Her eyes narrow. "Is it a boy?"

I smile, I can't help it. My phone buzzes in my hand but I resist the urge to look at it. "Kinda."

"Kinda," she mimics me. "I'd say definitely by the look on your face."

I wanna look at my phone so bad but Mum will kick off. I feel like it's literally burning my hand. "We just started talking."

"What's his name?"

Here come the questions. "Neymar."

"Where's he from?"

"London, but his parents are Trini."

I know she likes that. My mum is from Saint Lucia and has always wanted me to get with a fellow Caribbean. I hope she's asked all her questions because I want to read that message. She turns her attention to the pot and I unlock my phone in record time.

-Pussy wet?-

Fucking hell, I can practically hear him asking that question. *-Yes. R u hard?-*

"What does he do?"

I look up and she's staring again. I'm surprised she's allowed me to continue texting, she'd usually have the phone out my hand by now. "He owns a nightclub."

"And you like him?"

My phone buzzes and I smile, again. "Yeah."

She rolls her eyes and turns away. I'm straight on my phone.

-What u think? Is it home time yet?-

Ugh... no. Unfortunately. *-Not yet. Soon come.-*

"Okay, tell him goodbye and come help with the food," Mum says.

"Of course, Mum. Sorry."

I DRIVE TOWARDS HOME after dinner and all I can think about is Neymar. I'm well and truly obsessed. I need to call Eve as well.

"Call, Eve," I tell the cars sound system and it rings.

"About time," she answers.

"Sorry, Babe. Was at mums."

"Where are you now?"

"On my way home."

"So what happened last night?"

I smile... what didn't happen, that's the question. "Nothing."

"You're a terrible liar. You're ruined, aren't you?"

"Stop saying that, you've even got me thinking it."

"You are *so* ruined. Was it that good? Make you speechless, yeah?"

"You have no idea."

She giggles and I do, too.

"Anyway, what did you and Jay get up to last night?" I ask, diverting the topic away from me.

"Fuckin', drinkin', smokin', more fuckin'."

Damn. "Do you like him?"

"Come on now, Layla, you know I love my bad boys."

I shake my head. "You're terrible."

"I know, right. What you doing later?"

"Seeing Neymar."

"Oh, so it's Neymar again, now?"

I smile hard. It's always Neymar. "Yeah. What you doing?"

"I might see you later, I'm meeting up with Jay."

"Okay, I'm almost home."

"Okay, babe. In a bit," she says and hangs up.

I text Neymar as soon as I get in and tell him I'm home. He texts back straight away telling me he's on his way. I touch up my makeup and make a cup of tea while I wait. I know he wants to see me but I don't know what he wants to do so I hang fire on getting changed.

The door knocks and I let him in. He's in his usual dress code of black; jeans, shirt and jacket. He wears it well. His eyes burn me as he steps inside and my stomach flutters as I shut the door behind him.

I turn around and his lips are on mine. I give myself to him. I'm down for whatever he wants.

"You have no idea how good it feels to know I can do this to you now," he tells me between kisses.

He switches the hall light off and then turns me around so that my front is pressed to the door. He kisses my neck and I tilt my head to give him better access. I rest my forehead on my arm while his hands slip under my vest to scoop my breasts from out my bra. I gasp as he caresses them, teasing my nipples between his fingers.

"Did you miss me?" I ask with a smile.

"I guess you're about to find out." He roughly pulls my skirt up to my hips and my insides tighten. The anticipation of his actions is such a turn on...

I hear him rip the condom packet and my heart races. He's so bad, but I find it so fucking hot. His finger slips inside my thong and I gasp at his touch. I'm wet already and after wiping his finger on my ass cheek, I hear him unbuckling his belt and jeans. I part my legs a bit more and then I feel him shift my thong and start probing my entrance, lubricating himself.

I can't help but moan as he presses inside. *I'm still sore.* His hands find my hips and he drags me back and holds me firmly, entering me from behind and only stilling when he's hit my depths.

"Fuck, Layla, fuck." His breath is hot on my neck and my body shivers; there's just something about the way he says my name.

He slips a hand around to my front and after pushing past my thong, finds my most sensitive place. I inhale sharply at his touch before more moans escape me. *Oh. My. God.*

"Did you miss me as much as I missed you?" he asks huskily, stroking me to perfection.

"Y-es," I stutter and close my eyes. He gently sucks on my neck and then starts to move; dragging himself almost all the way out and then driving back inside. We are soon in sync and I meet him at every sharp thrust. My moans grow louder and he's groaning just the same. The sounds of our fucking, echo through my hallway. His thrusts become more urgent and my insides quiver, sucking him in. *So good...* My legs shake and I feel myself trembling with being so close to the edge.

"Your pussy is squeezing me so fucking tight," he says darkly.

I cry his name as I start to come, bucking back against him so he grinds deeper inside. I feel it everywhere, each wave like sparks of ecstasy. He calls my name and comes with me, holding my body so tightly that I never want him to let me go.

He leans his body on my back and kisses my neck. His sex is mind-blowing and I wonder how I'll ever get enough of it.

"So, you missed me, then?"

"All fucking day," he sighs. He pulls out and disappears to clean up. I adjust my thong, pull down my skirt and walk to the kitchen to find him.

"You're gonna kill me," I tell him and take a seat at the table. My legs are actually shaking and I'm not even exaggerating.

"Not if you don't kill me first."

He washes his hands in the sink and then steps over to me and kisses me hard on the lips. My eyes are still closed when he steps away and when I open them, he's staring at me.

"You're beautiful, you know that?" He sits beside me at the table while I blush at his unexpected compliment. He holds my hand and strokes his thumb over my fingers. "What do you wanna do tonight?" he asks after a while.

"What do you want to do?"

"I asked you first."

I narrow my eyes. "So?"

He rolls his eyes and I playfully scorn him. "Did you want to go out?"

"I don't mind." To be honest, I'd be happy staying in, under him all night. I can't get the sex out of my mind.

"I know what you're thinking," he says, staring at me deeply.

"I bet you do."

"I thought maybe we could double date it with your friend and Jay?" he suggests.

"Where?"

"At my new purchase."

"Eve will *love* that."

"I don't give a fuck about Eve. I wanna know what you wanna do."

Stay home and fuck?

"Don't worry, I fully intend to take advantage of you there, if we go."

"Is that so?" My insides tighten at the thought. "Text Jay. I'll get dressed."

CHAPTER 22

AFTER A QUICK shower, I dress in a red body-con. It doesn't have cut-outs, but it's fitted and shows the shape of my body perfectly. I tie my hair up into a quiffed ponytail and then go find Neymar in the kitchen.

"Do you want to stay home?" he asks when he sees me.

I smile and playfully roll my eyes. "Up to you."

"We better go now, before I change my mind."

We taxi it so no one has to drive. My heart doesn't race as badly when I walk into club Entourage this time, and I'm relieved. We go straight to the VIP to meet Jay and Eve and find them at the bar.

Eve hugs me. "Damn girl, is that one of your new dresses?"

"Yeah."

She gives me a kiss on the cheek but lingers to whisper in my ear. "I'm surprised you left the house."

"I know." I smirk as she steps away.

Neymar looks at me and I blush. I go from being confident around him one minute to nervous as hell the next.

"You wanna dance with me?" she asks.

"Have you ever known me to say no?"

I give Neymar a cheeky smile before hitting the dance floor with Eve.

The smile on my face as I dance to the music covers most of my face. Eve grins back at me, I bet she's thinking about Jay. I look over to our men standing by the bar and Neymar's expression makes my body shiver. I know what he's thinking about. He downs his drink and then my heart races as he walks towards me. *At least I can dance with him now and not be left sexually frustrated.*

My hand finds his and he spins me so my back is pressed to his front. He holds me close, snaking his hands around my body. I feel so happy inside, finally, he's mine.

I roll my hips; he's hard. It's like this man has a constant erection.

"I wanna fuck you," he says bluntly in my ear.

Turning in his embrace, I get lost in those eyes. "I want you to."

His eyes narrow before he grabs my hand and leads me to the elevator. He presses five on the keypad and when the doors close, he kisses me.

Once the doors re-open, he picks me up and my body clings to his as he walks forward.

"Where are we going?" I'm smiling hard.

"To my office."

"Am I in trouble?"

He gives me a quick chaste kiss. "You will be."

I stroke his neck with my fingers and he groans softly while pressing a code into a keypad. My heart flutters... damn, he's sexy.

We're quickly inside and after a few more strides he sets me down on his desk.

"You are damn sexy, Neymar." I look him over, he's so fucking strong my body craves him. "You turn me on bad."

"Layla." He parts my legs before stepping forward and then his lips are on mine. I pull his shirt out from his jeans and swiftly let him out. He pushes my dress up to my waist and then pulls me to the edge. His look is carnal and as his hand finds my chest, he pushes me back so I'm lying down.

My insides clench watching him pull out a condom and roll it on. Lifting my legs, he wastes no time in getting inside me. My eyes close as he fills me; he keeps giving me the best sex of my fucking life, I can't stand it.

He grasps my legs and guides them to his waist before pulling my hips against him. I gasp from how deep he reaches and tighten in protest.

"Fuck. Do that again," he demands.

He starts to move and I suck him in, tightening with every plunge of his dick. Moans involuntarily fall from my lips as he grinds himself in, reaching, filling me so fucking good I can't think.

I'm losing my mind with him.

"Layla, *fuck*."

My stomach flutters at hearing all that extra meaning.

He strokes my clit and I whimper his name. His grip on my legs becomes firmer; he drives in harder, repeatedly, building me up. I open my eyes and look at him and the look on his face rocks my soul.

I love him. *I love him so much.*

My legs tighten around his waist and I shudder as I start to come. He rests his body over mine and kisses me, muffling my cries of pleasure with his mouth.

"Layla," he whispers and with a final thrust, he comes. I don't think the sound he makes will ever leave my memory.

I hold him against me while the room is filled with our harsh breathing. He holds me tight with no hurry to compose himself but then suddenly I hear his phone ringing. I smile as I think about what Eve and Jay must be thinking right now. He nuzzles my neck and I moan as he rubs against me. Neymar is like a drug, a dangerously addictive one.

"Move in with me," he says abruptly.

My body tenses. "What?"

He kisses my shoulder and then lifts himself up so he can look at me. "Move in with me?"

I smile but I have no idea why. "You want us to live together? Already?"

He regards me closely but then smiles. "Yeah."

His phone rings again and his eyes dart in the direction of the sound before focusing back on me.

"It's probably Jay wondering where the hell we are," I tell him and can't help but smirk.

"Fuck him. You gonna move in with me? You'll be closer to work, and if you still get up at the same time, I can fuck you in the morning before you leave."

I exhale deeply at that. Morning sex with Neymar. Fuck yes. "Okay."

"Really?" I've surprised him.

I smile hard. "Yeah."

"Tomorrow?"

I nod. "Tomorrow."

CHAPTER 23

WE SORT OURSELVES OUT and his phone rings again.

He answers.

"What?" he shouts down the phone and then looks at me.

Something is wrong.

"I told you I wasn't on it and you're dragging me into it anyway, for fuck sake... I'm coming, just stay put." He shoves his phone in his pocket and grabs my hand. "I have to sort something."

I feel sick at his words because I know this has got something to do with his other life.

We hurriedly get Eve and Jay from the VIP and then make our way outside.

Jay is clearly a little drunk. "This isn't good, Jackson, we shouldn't go."

"I told you and Kimani to deal with that shit, now look?" Neymar is livid. I have to squeeze his hand for him to loosen his grip on mine. He turns to face me. "Will you and Eve be alright to taxi it home?" He's reluctant to go.

"Come with us?" I ask him quietly. "Please?"

I know I have no right to ask him that as soon as it leaves my lips, but I can see him fighting an internal battle; his eyes flickering between Jay and me before he sighs. "I can't."

He pulls me towards him and holds me tight. I don't want to let him go when he steps away. I can't ask him to come with us again, and I won't beg. I should never have asked him to stay in the first place because I have no right to. I knew the risks and I still let myself fall for him.

"I'll come to yours, after, okay?"

I nod because can't find my voice to speak. He kisses me quickly before getting in the back of a black BMW with Jay. We stare at each other through the window and I watch as the car drives away. Eve appears beside me and holds me around my shoulder.

"I don't like this, Eve."

"Me either."

AFTER DROPPING EVE OFF in the taxi, I go home. It's just after two when I get into bed. Checking my phone for news from Neymar, a heavy sigh escapes me.

Nothing.

I wish he hadn't gone. I'm so worried about him, he was so angry when he left and what I heard of his conversation; it didn't sound good.

I turn on the TV and clock-watch for an hour.

Still, nothing.

I wake to my phone ringing beside me.

"Eve?"

"Thank God, Layla, I've been calling you for ages." I can tell by the sound of her voice that something is very wrong. "Babe, Jackson got arrested."

My stomach turns at her words. "What?" I shout, sitting up in bed.

"Jay got away but Jackson didn't."

"What? So why didn't Jay fucking help him?"

"I'm sorr–"

"What station is he at?"

"Tooting."

"Where's Jay?"

"Here."

I check the time, it's six-thirty. "I'm coming over."

I feel sick all the way to Eve's house. *Oh God, Neymar.* What if he's in serious trouble? I know the police already want him for Deano's murder so they'll be wanting to pin anything they can on him for now.

Eve answers the door and I quickly get inside. "You heard anything yet?"

She looks guilty. "No, Hun. Nothing."

I check my phone, still nothing. I don't know if I'm expecting him to call me or not. *I hope he does.*

Following Eve into the living room, I see Jay texting on his phone. He looks up as we walk in. "Layla."

"Jay, tell me what happened."

He sighs. "By the time we got there, there was bare fighting. Jackson's boys and the East Side lot."

"Was he hurt?"

"No."

Thank God. "Doesn't he get a phone call?"

"Yeah, but he would've called Chris."

"Who's Chris?"

"His solicitor."

My emotions get the better of me and I have to turn away from them as I feel the tears coming.

"Hey," Eve says as she wraps her arm around me. "It will be okay."

"You don't know that," I snap and make my way to her kitchen.

After making a tea, I sit at the kitchen table. Tears fall and I wipe my face several times. I'm so worried, I wish he'd listened to me and not gone.

A phone rings in the living room before it's swiftly answered by Jay. I go to the door to listen.

"Yeah, it's Jay." He looks up at me and then looks away. "What? ... What with? ... Are you fucking serious? ... But he never did anything..." He gets up off the sofa and starts pacing. He looks and sounds angrier as the conversation continues. "So, just because he was there? ...What the fuck man!"

Eve comes to stand beside me and holds my hand. I hold it tight and feel my chest tightening. *This does not sound good at all...*

"So, what happens now? ... When can I see him? ... When is that gonna be?" Jay looks over to us but can't look at me in the eyes. My grip on Eve's hand tightens.

"Yeah." He hangs up and then angrily rubs his hands over his face. "They've charged him.

No... "What?"

"Charged him for some bullshit—Violent Conduct or something." He looks at Eve and then to me." They want him for something else but they can't prove it so they're doing him for this instead."

My legs give way and I fall to my knees, covering my mouth. They want him for Deano...

This is all my fault.

"Layla," Eve says, appearing down beside me.

"How long?" I ask Jay as I start to cry.

"Maximum..." He stops.

"How long, Jay?"

"Five years."

Gasping, I cough from catching my breath. Eve rubs my back and then she asks Jay if he thinks he'll get off.

"Chris doesn't think he will this time."

I cry harder.

"Can Layla see him?"

"No. He's in court Monday and then we'll find out more."

Eve holds me while I cry into her shoulder. *This is so bad... I knew it was too good to be true, I knew it wouldn't work. Oh, God...*

"I'm sorry, Layla," Jay says but his apology makes me angry.

Tearing myself away from Eve, I give Jay a lethal glare. "Sorry because he's in prison or sorry because you let him go? You knew he wanted out of that shit and you still let him go!" I get up from the floor while he tries to explain himself. "I don't want to hear it!" Oh god. My chest; it's pounding so hard, it hurts.

"Layla, it's not Jay's fault."

I glare at Eve and she flinches. Oh, I see how it is, I wonder how she would feel if it was Jay that was locked up.

"Let me know what time he's in court," I say coldly, walking to the door.

"Layla, wait," Eve calls while coming after me. Opening the door, I turn and face her. "I'm sorry," she says sympathetically.

I shut the door behind me.

"Everyone is always sorry."

CHAPTER 24

I BARELY MUTTER a hello to Johnny and the others when I get into work on Monday morning. Eve's been texting and trying to call me since I left hers yesterday but I haven't picked up. Kara and Kelly have called to ask how I am but I've kept the conversations short and just said I'm okay. I'm holding on to the little shred of hope I have left until the hearing later on at three.

My dad kept asking what was wrong when I saw him yesterday. Tears threatened but I managed to keep them inside but the dam broke when I got back home. As soon as I opened my eyes this morning my heart started aching all over again.

I told him not to go and now look at him... *look at us.*

"Hey," Maverick says, appearing beside my bench.

"Hey."

He looks nervous. "You okay?"

"I'm fine." I try to sound welcoming even though I feel like shit.

"I don't know if you've heard but Jackson's been arrested," he says quietly.

Neymar...

I narrow my eyes at him. "How do you know?" Was he there?

"I heard it from my boys yesterday. Everyone's talking about it. Looks like they want him for other stuff but they can only get him on Violent Conduct or rioting, or some shit."

"He didn't even do anything," I blurt out in his defence.

He looks at me suspiciously. "Layla–"

"Look, I know what you said about him, but he was trying to get out, trying to change." My voice falters and I have to bite my lip so I don't cry.

"Shit, Layla. You've been seeing him, haven't you? You're the girl that's got him so whipped."

"Whipped? What's that supposed to mean?"

"I heard he was giving up the streets for a girl."

I only just make it to my office before breaking down. I knew how much he wanted to leave that shit but I didn't realise it was because of me—not like that. Maverick walks in and after closing the door, wraps his arms around me.

"I know I was hard on you about him, I'm sorry."

"It's okay. I know I should have stayed away but I couldn't. I love him."

He rubs my back and sighs. "You want me to see if I can cover any of your appointments later?"

I pull back. "You know about that?"

"Everyone does. I'm assuming you want to go?"

"Yes."

"Alright. I don't approve, but, alright."

"Thank you."

I WALK INSIDE THE MAGISTRATES COURT at ten-to-three. My heart is pounding so hard. Eve and Jay are standing with a man in a suit but I don't go over to them. I lean against the wall and wait to be called in. This place brings back horrible memories of when my brother used to get arrested and I would have to lie to mum and say he was at a friends house when really he'd been remanded. I remember the day he got sent down for six months for possession of a Class B drug. I was so scared to go home and tell mum. *She went ballistic.*

"Babe?" Eve says, appearing beside me.

I don't look at her for long. "Yeah?"

"Jay spoke to Jackson last night."

I feel a deep stab of jealousy. *He didn't call me.* "What he say?"

"Uhm, well... he's pleading guilty."

"What?"

"Chris said he'd get less time."

"But he didn't do anything."

"I know, Hun. He did tell Jay something else..."

"What?" She's clearly scared to tell me.

"He kinda said... he didn't want you coming today."

"What?" *Oh my God, he said that?* My heart.

"He doesn't want to drag you into this."

What the fuck? "It's too late for that now, isn't it?" I hiss. I quickly look over to Jay but he's already staring at us. I return my focus to Eve. "I'm going in there."

"Maybe you–"

"I am going in there."

She nods and stays quiet. Jay comes over and she shakes her head at him.

"I am here you know." I glare at them both.

"Sorry," they both say, almost in unison.

A WOMAN CALLS NEYMAR'S CASE and we walk inside the courtroom. I stay beside Eve and Jay at the back of the room and stare at the half-glass, half-wooden box that Neymar will stand in when they bring him out. I feel a sharp pain in my chest. I want to believe that he'll get off but deep down...

A door to the right opens and my heart stops as I see him led in—handcuffed. I bite my lip to hold back my tears and I feel Eve slip her hand in mine. As if Neymar can feel me, he looks up and locks his eyes with mine. Even now I'm drawn to him and I feel my body move. His expression changes to one of disappointment? *Regret?* And then he looks away.

I stare at the side of his face while he stands in the box and the Judge comes in. The prosecution starts making their case but I can't look away from Neymar. I want him to look at me, I want him to acknowledge I exist. I know he's mad about what's happened, but I still need him.

"How do you plead?" I hear.

I hold my breath and squeeze Eve's hand, *not guilty, not guilty...*

"Guilty."

I gasp. "No," The judge stares and I recoil. Eve holds me around my back and I cry. *How could he? How could he just give in like that?* I look back at Neymar and he's staring at me. Tears fall down my face and I angrily brush them away. I shake my head as if to ask why but he just looks down at the ground before turning back to the judge.

He doesn't look at me again.

WE STAND OUTSIDE COURT. Eve stays silent while Jay chats on the phone.

He pleaded guilty? *Why?* Why didn't he fight it? Why didn't he fight to be out, with me?

"I don't get it, Eve," I say in a daze.

"Jay said he'd only serve half his sentence."

"But he didn't do anything."

"They wanted him for other things though, He had no choice."

"He *had* a choice."

"She's right," Jay says, sticking up for Eve. "Come, walk this way."

We follow him up the road to a park and while Jay stands, Eve and I take a seat on a wooden bench.

"Look, the police want him to do time. They know he's done stuff, they just can't prove it because he's too clever. I've never met anyone like Jackson, seriously, he's good at everything he does."

"But he should have pleaded not guilty."

"Think about it. He goes away now, he's out in two and a half years. He doesn't go away now and the police will just keep trying to put him away. The time away gets him away from the life that he hates, so this is good, Layla."

"How is that good?" My heart hurts so bad. "I can't live that long without him."

"Layla... listen, you're gonna have to let him go."

What? "Let him go?" No...

"The minimum he'll get is two and a half. He isn't gonna let you visit him inside."

"What? He said that?" *Neymar...* How could he do that to me?

Jay looks guilty but it only makes me feel worse. "He said he has to let you go."

"But, I love him." The words slip from my lips all on their own. I love him so much but he's hurting me so badly...

Jay is surprised but quickly moves on. "Sentencing is next week. Jackson doesn't want you there."

"He ... doesn't mean that."

"He does."

"I..." I can't do this.

Eve tries to grab my hand but I snatch it away and walk in the direction of my car. I call Maverick.

"Maverick?" I sob when he answers the phone.

"Layla, shit, are you alright?"

"Maverick ... it's so bad."

"Do you need me to come pick you up?"

"No, I'm gonna go home. Are you guys all okay there?"

"Yeah, we're good. Do you want me to come over after I lock up here?"

"No, I'll be in tomorrow." I can't let my customers down. "I'll see you when I get in."

"God, Layla. Are you sure?"

"Yeah."

"Okay. If you need anything, let me know, okay? I mean it."

"I will."

I LIE IN BED; my heart is breaking. If only I could turn back time and make him stay with me. Why is he cutting me off so hard? Didn't I mean anything to him? And what will even happen to the club, now? I thought that we were over the worst but this is so much worse than I could ever have imagined it could be. So much worse than what it was a few days ago and to make my life even more tragic, memories of him are everywhere; even laying here in my bed makes me feel sick.

THE WEEK PASSES SO SLOWLY; it's almost as though a minute takes a day. My mind is stuck in time, replaying the moments Neymar hugged me goodbye at the club and then the day he blanked me in court.

There's been no word from him and my hurt has started blurring with anger. How dare he treat me like this? It's like he's treating me as if I was just a one-fuck.

Eve thinks he's trying to save me, not wanting me to put my life on hold and wait for him, but I can't imagine being with anyone else. I feel so destroyed by him, the thought of living without him makes waking up in the morning unbearable. Never have I known pain like this, I feel as though my heart has been ripped out; nothing to look forward to, nothing to live for.

I STAND NEXT TO a pissed off Jay at the back of the Crown Courtroom. He begged me not to come, said that Neymar would kill him, but I don't give a fuck. I'm not deserting him, even if he seems to have deserted me. Neymar walks in handcuffed again but when I think he's going to look up at where we're sitting, he doesn't. He keeps his focus on the Judge, even though I know he wants to turn around.

"Neymar Harrison, you have pleaded guilty to Violent Disorder; Public Order Act 1986. As this is not your first offence, I am therefore sentencing you to the maximum of five years imprison—"

"No!" I sob. *Please no.*

"Bullshit," Jay says under his breath.

Neymar flinches.

Why won't he look at me? *Why?*

I turn to Jay, my anger overwhelming me. "You said he'd get half!" I seethe.

"That's what Chris said."

Tears fall down my face. "I fucking hate you!"

"Order!" the judge shouts, slamming his hammer down on his stupid fucking pedestal. I glare at him and angrily wipe away my tears.

"Fuck this!"

I hear him slam his hammer again but I barge past Jay and head to the door. Neymar looks behind and it stops me in my tracks. I see his hurt and take a step towards him but he turns away. I feel breathless from the hurt I feel and run from the room, making it to the steps outside just before I collapse and sob into my hands.

CHAPTER 25

EVE APPEARS by my side and she holds me as I cry. My body jerks with the strength of my cries. She hushes me but it makes me mad.

Abruptly I get to my feet and push her away. "Leave me alone!"

"Layla?" I can see her hurt but I turn and walk in the direction of my car.

I drive mindlessly until I find myself at Mums.

"Almighty, Layla, what is the matter?" she asks before she wraps me in her arms.

"Neymar, Mum... He's been sent... to prison for something, he didn't do anything."

"Calm down, Layla. I'll make us some tea."

She leaves me in the living room on the sofa before returning with our tea. She looks at me suspiciously and I know she's going to kick off when she finds out about what Neymar did.

"Come then," she says abruptly, "tell me what's going on."

So I tell her.

Everything.

Apart from Deano slapping me—and the night we met.

"If he won't talk to you," Mum says, "then there isn't much you can do. You must remember from when Dante was inside that he has to send you a visiting order if you have any chance of seeing him."

"I know." I feel so devastated.

"What does his friend say? Jay?"

"He's told me to forget about him, he didn't even want me going to court today. I know he's mad, Mum, I know he's angry, but I want to be there for him."

"But if he's away for five years then you can't put your life on hold. That's a long time."

"I don't care. I'll wait."

"Don't be silly. You don't even know if he'll still want to be with you when he gets out and if he doesn't, then it will all have been for nothing."

I physically recoil at that and wipe more tears from my face. I hate my life right now. "I'm not giving up on him, Mum. I can't."

WORK BECOMES A CHORE. I cut all contact with everyone and become a recluse. Work, home, sleep. Every day, on my way home from work I drive to Neymar's house and sit outside. I don't know why, he's been sent to Pentonville now, so it's not like he's coming home. *Five years.* I feel sick every time I think about it.

Maverick being the gem that he is managed to get me Neymar's prison number so I'm writing him a letter. He won't call me, that's fine, but if he thinks I'm giving up on him then he's got another thought coming.

Neymar.

I hope you're okay and this letter reaches you. Please let me come see you. Jay said you didn't want to me to come to court but I don't understand why? Why are you cutting me off? I thought we had something but you're treating me like I never existed.

I want to be here for you, I miss you. My life is so hopeless. I can't cope. Please, at least reply to this letter. Don't push me away. I know you're mad but I'm not mad with you.

You are killing me with this silence. Please.

I love you, Neymar.

Layla.

A month passes without a reply from Neymar. What did I do that was so bad?

Neymar.

I wrote to you over a month ago and you haven't replied – did you get it? If not, I just wanted to ask you to please stop ignoring me.

What did I do? Are you mad with me? I don't understand why you're cutting me off like this. I miss you. I don't even feel like myself anymore. I'm dying here, please. Write back to me at least. I'm going to keep writing until you do.

I love you.

Layla.

Another month goes by without a word. I'm at breaking point and I know something is going to have to give. I'm barely managing to make it through the day. I know deep down that I'm depressed and I should probably go to see the doctor, but I can't even be bothered to do that. I have absolutely no idea who I am, only that I am the shell of the person I used to be.

Neymar.

I know you're ignoring my letters. I've written to you twice now and I've checked your prison number. I just wanted to be here for you but you've dropped me like I was nothing. Talk to me, please. Send me a VO, let me come and see you. We can talk. I will wait for you if that's what you want. I love you so much. Please.

Layla.

I LOCK UP THE STUDIO AT SIX. I always think about Neymar, especially when I leave work. Memories of the first time I met him replay in my mind.

I feel like crying.

"Layla?"

Jay? I turn around. "What the fuck do you want, Jay?"

"Look, I know you don't want to talk to me..."

I turn away from him and head for my car. "Leave me alone."

"Layla, please, wait."

He runs in front of me and stops so I cross my arms before I look up at him. "What?"

"I need a word."

I think about the night Neymar took me away from Jason in the club. *'I need a word.'* "About what?"

"Jackson."

"What about him?"

"You have to stop writing him, Layla."

So, he's definitely been ignoring me. "That's none of your business."

"Yes, it is. He doesn't want you to."

That hurts. "What am I meant to do, Jay? I can't fucking cope! Why does he hate me so much?"

"He's doing the right thing, he's letting you move on."

"I don't want to move on! I fucking love him! I'm dying without him," I whisper.

"You're going to wait for him to get out?"

"If that's what he wants."

"It's not, though, he doesn't want you to. He wants you to move on. Forget about him, Layla. You're only hurting yourself by not letting go."

"But..." My heart breaks even more. I wipe the tears from my eyes and hear Jay sigh heavily.

"Look at you. You look..." he pauses. "...You need to move on, for your own sake."

"I can't," I sob, "I don't want to live anymore."

"Don't say that." He wraps his arms around me and I want to push him away but I don't. I cry hard into his chest. "Eve misses you, so does Kara and Kelly. You've cut everyone off because of him. We're all worried about you."

I pull myself away from him. "Well don't. I don't need any of your fucking pity."

"We don't pity you, we want to be here for you."

I lean back against the wall and sniff back my tears. What am I doing? I've become so weak, I've let Neymar consume me and now look?

I'm pathetic.

"I'll stop writing to him," I tell him, defeated.

Jay sighs with relief. "Thank you."

"What's happening with Entourage?"

"I'm running it, until Jackson gets out."

"And his house?"

"He owns it. I'm just keeping everything tickin' over."

"Hows Eve?" I hope she's okay. I do miss my girls.

"She's okay, she misses you. All the girls do."

I sigh. I need to sort my life out. "I'll call them."

He smiles sympathetically. "Good."

"How is he?" I ask quietly and his face hardens.

"He's alright. Angry, but okay. He's appealing the sentence."

"Really?"

"Layla, don't get your hopes up. He still wants you to move on, don't get any ideas."

That hurts. I nod and guilt takes over his face.

"So, should I tell Eve to expect a phone call?"

"Yeah. Give me a few days, okay?"

"Yeah. We're all here for you. I know I'm not your favourite person but I still don't like seeing you like this."

I nod. "See you around, Jay."

A FEW DAYS LATER after I get home from work, I make a cup of tea and then decide to call the girls. I need to speak to all of them really.

"Layla?"

"Hey, Kel'."

"How are you?" she gushes. It makes me feel bad.

"I'm okay, I guess. I saw Jay a few days ago. He told me to stop writing Neymar."

"You've been writing him?"

"Yea," I sigh. "I wanted to let him know that I was here for him, that I loved him."

"Did he reply?"

"No, and he got Jay to tell me to stop writing him, too."

"He did that?"

"Yeah. I feel so hopeless. Jay said I have to move on, forget about him basically, but I feel as if Neymar's my soul mate. He's everything I see, Kel', I don't know how to get over him."

"Oh, Babe. I don't know what to say. You can't force him to talk to you and you can't carry on like this. You're becoming a stranger. In all the years we've been friends, this is the longest we've gone without talking."

"I know. I know."

"But I understand. I don't know what I'd do if anything happened to Jack."

"Yeah, well, we're friends and I want to be there for you, especially with the baby. I bet you have a bump now and everything."

"I do. I miss you, could we meet up soon?"

"I'm going to call the others, I'll arrange something. Lunch on Saturday, maybe, if everyone is free."

"That would be so nice, Hun."

"I'll text you, okay? I should call Kara."

"Okay. I love you."

"Love you, too."

"Bye."

"Layla?" Kara answers.

I roll my eyes, the tone in these girl's voices; you'd think they were talking to a ghost. "Hey, Babe."

"Layla, oh God, it's so good to hear your voice."

I've been a shit friend. "I know, Hun, I'm sorry."

"Don't you dare be sorry. I just want to be there for you, I love you so much."

"I'm sorry. I just don't know what to do, I'm not coping one bit."

"Oh, Babe. Let's get together, soon."

"I've spoken to Kelly; are you free this Saturday? For lunch?"

"I'm going to Danny's mums but I can work around that, just let me know times and I'm there."

"Okay, Hun, I will. Thanks for talking to me."

She scoffs. "Don't be silly. I'd love you no matter what. We're sisters, aren't we?"

"Yeah. I'll text you after I speak to Eve."

"Okay."

I look at Eve's number on my phone screen. What do I even say to her? I love her but I can't help feeling like she knows more about Neymar's situation than I do. It hurts. Jay got away that night and Neymar didn't. I think deep down, I resent her. I don't want to and I really shouldn't feel like this but I can't help it. I should just be honest with her. Ugh... I tap the call button. My heart races while it rings.

"Layla."

"Eve."

The silence is awkward. I hear her sigh.

"I'm sorry."

Sorry? "What for?"

"For everything that's happened. For trying to stop you going to court, for that night."

"It wasn't your fault."

"I dunno. I feel like everything got so messy after Jackson, y'know, went inside."

"I know."

"I feel so guilty. If it wasn't for you then I wouldn't have met Jay, and now I have Jay and you don't..."

"Have Neymar." I can feel tears threatening and sigh heavily. "It's not your fault. It's mine really. Something happened and I think it's my fault why he felt the need to plead guilty to that violent disorder."

She doesn't say anything and I realise it's probably because she already knows.

"He doesn't want me writing him, he doesn't want any contact with me. Jay is right. I have to forget him, even if it's just for my own sanity. I don't even recognise myself."

"Oh, Babe," she sobs and it makes the pooled tears fall from my eyes. "I just wish I could do something to take your pain away. I feel so awful over it all."

"Honestly, I feel like you kinda know more about what's going on with Neymar than me, I think I sort of resent you for it."

"No, girl, I completely understand that. I mean, if I was you, I would feel the same."

"I don't want to feel like that though, Eve, I hate myself for feeling like this."

"Meet me sometime, please? We can talk, face to face."

"Kelly and Kara said they can meet for lunch on Saturday, if you're free?"

"Of course. Name a time and place and I will be there."

"What about the Grill. One o'clock?"

"Sure. Do you want to get a few drinks afterwards?"

"We'll see. I just want to see you all first."

"Of course. Okay, well, I'll see you Saturday?"

"Yes, Hun."

CHAPTER 26

I TAKE A DEEP breath before I walk into the grill. My nerves are getting the better of me, I can't remember the last time I felt so nervous. Actually, yes I can.

It was around Neymar.

Oh, God...

George frowns when he sees me but quickly smiles after. The girls are sitting at a table to the left and I smile meekly at them before grabbing a double Henny at the bar. It's strong but I need some courage right now.

"Hey," I say to the girls when I reach them. They reply with a chorus of *'hey's'* while I pull out a chair and sit down. They regard me closely. It's because I look different.

"Should we order some food?" Kara suggests with wide eyes.

"Layla, when is the last time you ate something?" Kelly asks carefully. The look of horror on her face strangely hurts and I look down at my fingers from shame. I have no idea, I've just been surviving on coffee. I shrug.

"I don't want to upset you, Hun, considering we're only just talking again but girl, I have never seen you look so slim."

I shrug again. Eating hasn't really been on my list of things to do but by the look on their faces, I must have lost more weight than I thought.

Kelly's hand reaches for mine and I look at her. "Should we get some barbecue?" she asks.

She looks so hopeful that I can't bear to say no. "Yeah."

Smiling with relief, she nods. "We'll get a platter to share between us," she says before disappearing to find George at the bar to order.

An uncomfortable silence falls over the table now that Kelly has gone. My heart races, I should say something but I don't know what.

"So, how's work?" Kara asks.

I tuck some hair nervously behind my ear. I can answer that question... "Busy. I need a bigger place actually. I've been looking at a few premises in central."

"That's good," Kelly says, returning.

"Yeah. I guess it would be good to have a fresh start somewhere." Especially because there are so many memories of Neymar at my current place. *Don't think of him here...* "Kara, I'm sorry I missed your birthday."

"You didn't miss anything. Danny and me went up to Manchester for the weekend."

I nod. "Did you have a good time?"

"Yeah, it was really nice. Danny is just so..." Her thoughts clearly drift but it's as if she remembers something bad and then the look of regret she gives me irks me.

"Hey, I'm happy for you guys," I lie. They all have their men and I have nothing.

"I bought my scan picture with me, would you like to see it?"

The smile that takes my face is genuine and it feels good to feel good, even if the feeling is fleeting. "Of course I do."

She takes out a white card from her bag and hands it to me. I smile when I open it. The tiny black and white figure of a baby warms my heart. "I still can't believe you are actually having a baby."

"Neither can we," Eve says.

"Do you think you'll have a boy or a girl?" I ask when handing her back the image.

"I'd like a boy, Josh wants a girl. We've decided to move the wedding forward as well, we're thinking in a few months."

"Okay, just let me know."

"Of course, we'll have to have some dress fittings."

I nod and feel my mood slipping again but I'm saved when the barbecue platter arrives. My stomach growls when I see my favourite food, I am hungry.

We eat mostly in silence. Kara informs me that she has a new job and Eve got a promotion so she now runs the entire advertising team at her work. I feel proud of my girls, they are all making such progress in their lives. Me, however...

"Is that all you're eating?" Eve asks accusingly.

"I'm full."

"Eve," Kelly scorns. "She probably has such a small stomach now."

I roll my eyes; Kelly, always such the grown up. She is going to make such an amazing mother. The thought makes me jealous, Neymar wanted kids...

"How are you feeling?" Kara asks as if she can read my mind.

"Shit." I shrug.

"We get that. I... we are just so worried about you."

"I know and I'm sorry I cut you all off." I sigh heavily. "Jay told me that Neymar doesn't want me to wait for him..." I glance at Eve and she looks guilty. "...Practically begged me to leave him alone."

"Would you wait?" Kelly asks tentatively.

"I would, if he wanted me to. I love him and I don't think I will love anyone else the same way—but, like Jay said, I can't force Neymar to speak to me so I have to let him go."

"Well that's easier said than done, isn't it?"

"Yeah. I just wish I could erase it all from my memory. It's just so hard," I whisper. Don't cry...

"Time, Babe," Kelly says, reaching for my hand. "Just give it time, let us be here for you, anything we can do, we're here for you."

I nod as I hold back my tears. "I know."

When I get home, I lie in bed and stare at the ceiling. I have to let him go but I don't want to. Jay said not to write to Neymar again but I want to so bad, even just to say that I'll leave him alone. I don't really want to get Jay into shit with him either. I need something to get over this.

My mind drifts again, to the car park, to Deano. The thought of what he did being the reason he's inside, it's eating me up. If only I never opened my mouth, if only he hadn't brought me that soup that night, he would never have known and we'd still be together. It's my fault and really I have no one to blame except myself.

I wake from another dream about him. I wipe my face. I've been crying in my sleep again.

The thought of going to my dads for the day, makes me sigh. My life is such a failure, it's like I've completely fallen apart since he went away. I can't keep living like this.

After having a cold shower, I moisturise my body and look at my tattoo in the mirror. Memories of Neymar and this tattoo overwhelm me again. I sit on my bed and cover my face in my hands. What am I going to...

A tattoo.

I could get a tattoo. A sleeve. I could put his tattoo on my arm. That way, he will always be with me, even if he doesn't want to be. Excitement rushes through me, I'll get Marco to ink me. I think I still have Neymar's sketches somewhere. I could redesign something.

I sit at my desk with a cup of tea and the sketch of Neymar's tattoo. I start drawing a layout for a sleeve; I'll get it on my left arm; the angel at the top, then the pool underneath. Maybe a smaller wolf wrapped around my forearm and then I just need something for the underside. I could give the angel longer hair, maybe so it flows to wrap around my arm.

That's it. I stare at the sketch, this is it. Just one final thing. The date I met him on my wrist. It will always remind me of him but this is what I need, a permanent reminder that we were something at one point in time. I won't ever regret meeting him, although I wish things ended differently.

MY ALARM WAKES ME for work on Monday morning and for the first time in months, I can't wait to get to work.

Once I get to the shop, I ignore Johnny and find Marco. He's with a customer but I don't care. "Marco?"

He raises his foot from the pedal of his machine and regards me cautiously. "You okay?"

"I need you to ink me, asap. Let me know when you can fit me in?"

He looks confused but nods. "Sure."

I smile before I leave him with his customer and find my station.

This is good, positive. This can be my therapy... The pain of being inked will help me. I don't know what else I can do to forget him so this way my skin can wear him and I can hopefully move on.

Maverick appears at my station just after lunch. "Hey, Layla."

"Hey."

He smiles and tilts his head. "You seem, different."

I feel more positive. "Yeah. I want to speak to you all before I leave today."

"Everything okay?"

"Yeah." I haven't told them I want to move the salon.

"Alright, no worries."

I see out the last customer and the boys sit at their usual places and I lean against the door.

"Thanks for staying, I'll make this quick. Firstly, I want to say sorry to all of you. The last few months I have been unbearable at times and quite frankly, a full-blown bitch," They look at me knowingly. "Thanks for being patient with me and I hope you can forgive me for all my bullshit."

"You've been there for all of us, a few months of you treating us like shit can be forgiven," Johnny says, smirking his head off.

I roll my eyes. "Thanks, I don't need a lawsuit, especially because... I'm thinking of moving us to a bigger place."

"Hell yeah, that means a bigger desk for me," Johnny jokes.

"Are you serious?" Marco asks surprised.

"Yeah. How would you guys feel about moving to a bigger studio and taking on a couple more artists?"

"I'm game," Maverick answers quickly.

Marco agrees. "Where are you thinking?"

"Somewhere more central, I'll have to speak to the bank, but with the money we've been making, I can't see it being a problem."

"I think it's a sick idea," Marco says. "We could definitely do with a bigger place."

I'm relieved. "Good. We can all go view some premises together, if you guys want to come with?"

They all agree.

"Okay, well, that's all. Marco, have you had a look at your schedule yet?"

"Yeah. I have half a day next Wednesday free if that's any good for you?"

"Johnny? Do you think you could work your magic and free me up for then? I can work earlier or later if you can rearrange my appointments?"

"I'm sure I can do that. Leave it with me."

This is good. Really good.

"Is that a smile I see?" Maverick comments.

"I think it is." I smile harder. "Johnny, let me know asap, yeah?"

"I will."

IT'S WEDNESDAY and I'm in Marco's chair. I'm holding my sketch so tightly in my hands. I'm nervous.

"So, your sleeve, you finally decided what you want."

"Yeah," I reply quietly.

"Let me see, then."

I hand him the sketch and watch a frown take his face. He knows.

"You always give your customers a lecture when they ask for ink like this, Layla. You sure about this?"

His eyes search mine but I've made up my mind. I need to do this. "I'm sure."

"Okay," he says casually. "Top off, then."

I pull my t-shirt off and sit back in his chair in just my leggings and bra. I take a deep breath; I'm nervous as hell but I need this to move on. I can make what we had real, carry him with me, put him on my body permanently. Then, hopefully, I can get past this.

Marco wipes down my arm and adjusts his stool. I watch him intently, remembering when he did my thigh piece. I love his work. He's quiet and I know he's thinking so hard in that head of his.

"Hows Emily?" I ask to disrupt his thoughts.

"She's okay."

"And the baby?" I whisper.

"All good so far. We'll find out the sex next week."

"And are you going to stay with her?"

He sighs. It's a troubled one. "I don't know. For the moment, yeah. Things have been good and the thought of having a family of my own is making me want to stay with her."

"Make sure you stay with her for the right reasons, though, Marco."

"I know. We'll see."

I nod and he gives me a crooked smile in response. He fixes some new needles to his machine and looks at my sketch again.

"Are you definitely sure about this?" he asks before he dips his needle in the ink.

"Yes."

"Alright."

I close my eyes and hear the leather creak as I lean back in his chair. I feel the first scratch of the needle and sigh.

Neymar...

I remember how I felt so nervous working on his body for the first time... And the way he moved underneath me... our first kiss... those lips... My stomach sinks and the regret takes hold. The memories are so vivid I could touch them. It hurts so bad that a tear falls from my eye and I feel Marco still.

"You okay?" he asks tentatively.

"I'm good," I reply quietly, keeping my eyes shut. This is my therapy, this is me moving on. I'm the shell of the person I used to be because of him. I need to do this.

"YOU'RE DONE."

I've been in Marco's chair for six hours.

My sleeve is finally done and I feel *relieved*. He hands me a mirror and I turn my body to see my sleeve. *It's perfect.* The angel's eyes follow me as I turn my arm and I feel a rush of happiness at having it on me.

"Thank you. It's exactly what I needed."

He's full of pride. "If I do say so myself, it's a beast of a tattoo."

"It is." Oh, God, I love it. The Angel looks exactly like Neymar's. "How much do I owe you?"

"Nothing."

"What?"

"It was worth it, just to see you like this again."

"Marco, no. You can't not charge me."

"I can and I am."

I narrow my eyes at him. That's fine. I'll just slip it into his cut over the next few months. "Thank you, Marco."

Johnny and Maverick appear and look at my arm with inquisitive eyes. I can see the recognition on Maverick's face but Johnny appears clueless.

Mavericks eyes find mine and we have a silent passing of words before he nods. "So is the old Layla making a comeback?"

"Give me time, but I think so."

CHAPTER 27: NEYMAR

'I love you...'

"Fuck sake!"

"What's up, buddy? You get some bad news? I hate when that happens."

I stare down my dirty looking cell mate lying in the bunk opposite mine. *Shut the fuck up.*

'*...you just dropped me like I was nothing...*'

No, Layla, you're everything, that's why I have to let you go. This fucking woman makes me wanna cry I swear down.

"It's okay if you wanna cry, mate. We all do."

I ignore him. I wish he'd fuck off. This guy never shuts up. I need to speak to Jay, to see if he's spoken to Layla yet. I need her to stop writing me letters.

Being in here—without her, it's hard enough.

I CUT THE QUEUE to the payphones to call Jay.

"Yes, Boss," he answers.

Don't be bait... "How's the club?"

"Making you bare P."

At least I'll get out to money... "Good. Did you speak to Chris?"

"Yeah. He sounds pretty certain he can sort you getting out after half."

"Tag, though, man." Fuck being on tag... I want him to find a flaw in the evidence so I can get out clean.

"Better than staying inside, bro, but you might not."

"Yeah."

"So, I spoke to, Layla, yesterday."

Layla. So he's seen her. "How is she?"

"Fucking skinny, man. She really ain't coping. Are you sure you're doing the right thing? She says she wants to wait for you to get out. I don't wanna overstep, but she ain't good at all."

I glare at the bunch of pussies in the queue for the phone and they quieten down. I didn't wanna hear that. I know from her letters I'm hurting her bad, and I promised no one would ever hurt her again. I'm hurting her nuff. "I'm sure. I can't make her wait. She deserves better."

He sighs. "Alright, man. Well, I told her to stop writing. She said she was gonna ring the girls so hopefully they'll be able to look after her."

"Good. Sooner she moves on the better. I know how close she is to her friends, she'll be alright."

"Whatever you say, boss."

"Yeah. In a bit."

"Cool."

Fuck.

The thought of her hurting is getting to me. She don't need someone like me fucking her life up. I should've listened when she told me to go home with her. Everything was always good when I was with her.

Fuck sake!

I fucking love her, but I fucked it all up so bad. Getting Entourage was supposed to make everything okay to move to her but I still found a way to fuck it up. Story of my life. I don't know why I thought that it could work out with her. Nothing ever works out the way I want it to.

I could never be that lucky.

And now the thought of her moving on, someone else touching her body makes me murderous but I can't be selfish, I can't do that to her.

This is my fault, not hers.

I should never have messed with her.

Fucking five years.

Fucking bullshit.

At least it's not life.

Deano and all of them deserved it.

I'd do Deano again.

Nothing would ever be too much for that woman. Maybe I *should* make her wait. I know she would, even for the fact she's just too nice for her own good.

Nah, I can't do that to her. She deserves to be happy.

Fuck sake, Layla.

One year later...

Neymar.

I know you don't want me to write to you, I promise this is the last time – don't be mad with Jay.

How are you? I hope it's not too bad in there... I moved my studio. I'm in Central now, my new place has two floors, it's so much bigger. I've had to take on more staff as well and we are busier than ever. There's no way I'd be able to fit you in for ink now...

Kelly got married and she's had her baby. She had a little girl and she's beautiful. The christening is next week.

I was really just writing to tell you that I've met someone.

I wish things could have been different between us but only you know why they couldn't be.

Take care, Neymar.

I love you.

Layla.

-END OF PART ONE-

Other books by this Author

A Christmas Wish: Santa and his Candy Cane
A Paranormal Holiday Novella

The Perfect Waters Series
An African American Mermaid Paranormal.

The Abriya & Clarence Series
Becoming Aware (Book 1 & 2)
Anarchy (Book 1 & 2)
Eternity. (The Finale)
A Complete Urban Paranormal Romance Series.

Awakening Ariella James. An Abriya & Clarence Series Spin-off (Book 1 & 2)
Taming Harmony James. An Abriya & Clarence Series Spin-off (Book 3)
A Complete Urban Paranormal Romance Series.

The Lands of Aurellia & Caro. Battle of the Pires. The Kratius Series (Book 1, 2 & 3)
A Complete Urban Fantasy Romance Series.

The Roadman (Part 1 & 2)
A Complete Urban Romance Series.

Near But Yet So Far (Standalone)
An Urban Billionaire Love Story.

Dear Destiny. The Letter Chronicles. (Standalone)
An Urban Romance.

Dear Cherish. The Letter Chronicles. (Standalone)
An Urban Romance.

Chasing the Sun: A Summer of Love and Hate.
Urban Romance Anthology
Features the pre-novelette to Captured Love (*Coming Soon*)

Just an Escort (Standalone)
A Contemporary Erotic Romance.

Follow me on Facebook on my personal page or readers group for bonus chapters, new releases and sneak peeks.

Please leave a review of this book if you can, it really does help.

Want to give me your review personally? Then please come and talk to me...

Reader's Group – https://goo.gl/mPQ8XD
Facebook Profile – https://www.facebook.com/leesha.mccoy.7
Facebook Like Page – https://www.facebook.com/authorleeshamccoy
Instagram – https://www.instagram.com/leeshamccoyauthor
Twitter – https://twitter.com/LeeshaMcCoy
Goodreads – https://goo.gl/RLJTDR

You can sign up to my mailing list here: https://goo.gl/c9rcMy

About LeeSha McCoy

LeeSha McCoy is an African American Romance writer. She released her first book in 2012 and currently writes Urban Romance, Paranormal, Fantasy & Contemporary. She always writes about strong women and her mission is to write books for everybody, frequently blending the lines between genres.

Writing novels that make her readers feel is something she prides herself on. She doesn't just write stories to be read, but for her readers to experience.

She began writing in the late 90's, although it was mostly song lyrics she wrote to escape her loneliness. As one of only a handful of bi-racial children living in her small hometown of Banbury, she struggled to make friends and to be accepted, so she spent most of her childhood alone.

She currently lives in Milton Keynes, England, but the American half of her family is spread across the United States, including Baltimore, Colorado and Texas.

A wife and Mother to four beautiful children, LeeSha spends her spare time caring for her family or binge reading steamy romance novels.

Printed in Great Britain
by Amazon

14430479R00089